# J. T. EDSON'S
# FLOATING OUTFIT

The toughest bunch of Rebels that ever lost a war, they fought for the South, and then for Texas, as the legendary Floating Outfit of "Ole Devil" Hardin's O.D. Connected ranch.

**MARK COUNTER** was the best-dressed man in the West: always dressed fit-to-kill. **BELLE BOYD** was as deadly as she was beautiful, with a "Manhattan" model Colt tucked under her long skirts. **THE YSABEL KID** was Comanche fast and Texas tough. And the most famous of them all was **DUSTY FOG**, the ex-cavalryman known as the Rio Hondo Gun Wizard.

J. T. Edson has captured all the excitement and adventure of the raw frontier in this magnificent Western series. Turn the page for a complete list of Berkley Floating Outfit titles.

## J. T. EDSON'S
## FLOATING OUTFIT
## WESTERN ADVENTURES
## FROM BERKLEY

# J.T. Edson

# THE COLT AND THE SABRE

BERKLEY BOOKS, NEW YORK

Originally published in Great Britain
by Brown Watson Ltd.

This Berkley book contains the complete
text of the original edition.
It has been completely reset in a typeface
designed for easy reading, and was printed
from new film.

THE COLT AND THE SABRE

A Berkley Book/published by arrangement with
Transworld Publishers Ltd.

PRINTING HISTORY
Corgi edition published 1968
Berkley edition/November 1986

ISBN: 0-425-09341-7

A BERKLEY BOOK® TM 757,375
Berkley Books are published by The Berkley Publishing Group,
200 Madison Avenue, New York, New York 10016.
The name "BERKLEY" and the stylized "B"
with design are trademarks belonging to
Berkley Publishing Corporation.
PRINTED IN THE UNITED STATES OF AMERICA

# CHAPTER ONE

## Miss Boyd Prepares to Leave

Up at the big house, taken over by the 6th New Jersey Dragoons' officers as their mess, a ball was in progress. Music, laughter, the hum of conversation, clink of glasses and clatter of plates came faintly and annoyingly to Private Hooley's ears as he stood guard on the stables which housed the pick of the officers' horses. After over an hour on the duty, Hooley found the noise growing increasingly more distasteful. More so when he knew that all but the essential men on guard detail celebrated news of a United States Army victory over the rebels back east.

When Hooley enlisted in the Dragoons, filled with patriotic fervour, he expected to spend all his time alternating between charging and routing the grey-clad enemy and being fêted by the adoring civilian population. Instead he found himself sent to Arkansas, where he learned foot-drill, how to ride a horse in a mighty uncomfortable fashion, dismount and prepare to fight on foot, perform the essential military task of kitchen-police and stand guard

1

duty. None of them pleasant or attractive to a man who looked for high adventure; and of them all, he cared least for standing guard. A two-hour stretch on the stable post could stretch on and on until it felt more like two hundred. Especially when, like tonight, the brass could be heard celebrating and being fêted by what passed in the Bear State for an adoring civilian population.

A shape approached the stables, coming from the rear of the big house. From the white cap, black dress, white apron and the fact that the approaching woman carried two traveling bags, Hooley deduced that she must be a servant to one of the fancy, high-toned gals attending the ball. He could tell little about the woman's figure or face, for a maid's uniform did not tend to emphasize its wearer's shape and so far she had not entered the limited area of light from the stable door.

"Howdy, gal," he greeted, it sounding better than lining his Springfield carbine and calling the formal "Halt, who goes there?"

"Howdy, you-all," answered the girl, her voice husky and holding a hint of a southern drawl. "Just bringing these bags down for my mistress. She's going to have Captain Haxley take her home. Only the good Lord knows when that'll be. And I've got to stay here and wait for her."

At that moment the girl entered the patch of light. She stood maybe five feet seven in height and, despite the limitations of her clothes, gave the impression that she could show a mighty pretty figure dressed more suitably. The white cap hid all her hair, but Hooley did not give a damn for that as he studied her face. Hooley prided himself on his judgment of women, and he decided that the girl before him was about as beautiful as he had ever seen. Taking in the almost faultless features, the long-lashed dark eyes, the slightly upturned nose, Hooley's main attention rested on the full lips and their warm, inviting smile. If Hooley knew anything about women—and he would modestly admit that he knew plenty—that girl wanted company real bad.

"Got to wait down here?" he asked.

"Sure have," she agreed, halting by the door and setting down the bags. They were made of good leather and designed to strap on to a saddle; not the usual kind of luggage a lady of quality used when traveling, although Hooley ignored the point.

"Could get mighty lonesome," he remarked, glancing around to make sure that nobody observed him.

"It surely does," answered the girl. "Say, does this stable have a golden horseshoe nail?"

Knowing what the girl meant, Hooley fought down an anticipatory gulp. Even after only a year in the Army, he knew the legend of the golden horseshoe nail and its use in luring members of the opposite sex into the privacy of a stable.

"Sure it does," he said and hoped his voice did not sound as husky to her ears as it came to his.

"Sergeant Papas was going to show it to me," the girl explained, "but he's not been around to see me."

That figured, thought Hooley, for Papas held post as sergeant of the guard. No love being lost between Hooley and Papas, the private figured showing his sergeant's prospective prey the "golden horseshoe nail" might be highly diverting. Having made a study of such matters, Hooley knew that the officer of the day would be most unlikely to make rounds while the dance ran its course and, without prodding by his superiors, Papas never left the guard house when on duty.

"Come on inside," he grinned. "I'll show it to you."

Entering the stable, lit by a solitary lantern hanging over the door, Hooley rested his carbine against the door and looked around him. Some twenty horses stood in the line of loose stalls around the walls. A rack supported McClellan army saddles at one side of the room. Hooley ignored both sights, his attention being on the ladder which led up to the hay loft. Did he have time to take the girl up there, or should he show her the "golden horseshoe nail" in the less comfortable confines of an empty stall?

While Hooley pondered on that important problem, the girl opened the vanity bag which had hung from her wrist and been obscured by the travelling bag in her hand. Taking out a silver hip-flask, she threw a dazzling smile at the soldier. As she came towards him, he caught a whiff of perfume. Not the brash, cheap kind poorer girls mostly used, but something more subtle and expensive. If Hooley thought of the matter at all, he put the aroma down to the maid helping herself to her employer's perfume. Such a trivial detail never entered Hooley's mind, it being fully occupied with thoughts of forthcoming pleasure and interest in the contents of the flask the girl offered to him.

"I sneaked this out of the house," she told him. "Got it filled up with some of the best I could find."

Taking the flask, Hooley removed its stopper and sniffed at an aroma even sweeter to his nostrils than the perfume the girl used. He had never come across so fine a smelling whisky and forgot his manners. Tilting the flask, he drank deeply, making no attempt to let the girl precede him. The whisky bit his throat and burned warmly as he sucked off what would have been a good four-fingers drink in the post sutler's store—and better whisky than that shrewd trader ever offered the enlisted men at that. Having drunk, his thoughts turned to other matters. Gallantly he rubbed the top of the flask and offered it to the girl.

"How about you?" he inquired as she replaced the stopper.

"Shuckens, a girl doesn't drink strong liquor," the girl giggled. "I only brought it out in case I met a handsome gentleman who looked thirsty."

"You've got a real kind heart, gal," Hooley declared, feeling his spirits rise as the whisky sank warmingly into his belly.

"I sure have," she agreed, placing the flask back into her bag. With her hand still inside the bag, she suddenly stiffened and stared in a horrified manner at something behind him. "Look out!" she gasped.

Hooley spun around, not knowing what might be waiting for him. Even as he began to turn, he saw a change come to the girl's face. No longer did it hold either warm invitation or startled fear, but a cold, determined expression transformed her beautiful features. Before the change could register in Hooley's mind, he had completed his turn. A sudden dizziness whirled up inside Hooley, although it did not last for many seconds.

Holding a short, lead-loaded, leather-encased billie, the girl's hand emerged from her bag and whipped around in the direction of Hooley's head. While many regiments of the U.S. Army now tended to standardize their equipment, the New Jersey Dragoons retained their traditional uniform. The buff-colored trimmings of the uniform, differing from the more general cavalry yellow, made a handy conversational piece in a bar; and the peaked, soft-crowned cap was claimed to be far more comfortable than the "Jeff Davis" or Burnside hat now issued to other regiments. However, the cap offered no protection against the sun or an attack on the base of the skull. Coming around with a snappy flick of the wrist, the billie caught Hooley's head just under the rim of the hat and he crumpled forward, collapsing to the floor without a sound.

"Sorry, soldier," the girl said, her voice still husky and "deep south," but bearing the accent of an educated, cultured upbringing. "They do say showing the golden horseshoe nail to a girl weakens a man. And I reckon you'd rather have your brass think you'd been jumped from behind than know you'd taken a drugged drink."

Even while speaking, the girl returned her billie to the vanity bag, bent and gripped Hooley's ankles to drag him aside so he would not be visible from the door. Leaving the soldier, she went straight to the stall housing the colonel's favourite horse, a big, fine-looking bay gelding noted for its stamina and speed. Collecting a saddle from the rack, the girl carried it to the bay's stall. There she removed her cap, exposing almost boyishly short hair so black that it seemed to shine blue in the lamp's light. Next she unfastened and wriggled out of the maid's dress. Even had Hooley been conscious to witness the disrobing, he would have met with disappointment. Instead of emerging dressed in underwear, the girl proved to be clad in a man's dark blue shirt, tight-legged black riding breeches and high-heeled riding boots with spurs on their heels. An opportunity to caress her hips while she wore the maid's dress would have handed Hooley a surprise, for she wore a gunbelt with an ivory-handled Dance Brothers Navy revolver, butt forward in the open-topped holster at her left side.

Leaving her discarded clothing on the floor of the bay's stall, the girl began to saddle the horse. She worked fast, handling the baby deftly despite its reputation for being awkward and mean. With her chosen mount saddled, she led it to the barn's door and fastened it just inside. Collecting another saddle from the rack, she went again to the stalls. This time she selected and saddled a powerful roan, the pride of the major commanding Company D, leading it to the side of the bay.

For a moment the girl stood by the barn's door, listening to the sounds of revelry which came from various parts of the camp. She saw nothing to disturb her, no sign of approaching authority; which did not entirely surprise her as she had been at the ball and seen the officer of the day enjoying himself in a manner which made his attending to duty an unlikely possibility.

"I hope the boys do their part," she mused, returning to release the remaining horses.

On being freed, each horse made its way towards the door of the barn and passed out into the darkness. Outside they began to bunch, uncertain of what course to follow. After turning loose the last horse, the girl went and dragged Hooley outside. Her blow had stunned him, but the laudanum in the drink she gave him served to keep him quiet long after the effects of the blow wore off. Another quick glance around and the girl entered the barn once more. Taking down the lantern, the girl carried it to the stall where her clothing lay. She hurled the lantern against the wall. Glass shattered, oil sprayed out and flames licked up, bounding across the straw. Calmly the girl waited until she felt certain that her discarded clothing would be consumed by the spreading flames, then she ran to the two saddled horses. Already the roan's reins were secured to the bay's McClellan saddle. The horses moved restlessly as the flames began to lick up and grow in fury. Showing considerable skill, the girl swung astride the bay and urged it out into the night, the roan following, obedient to the gentle pull of the reins.

Drawing her revolver, the girl rode towards the freed horses. "Yeeah!" The ringing yell of the Confederate cavalry burst from her lips and she fired a shot into the air.

Startled by the yell and shot, the horses began to run. Letting out another wild yell, the girl urged her mounts after the departing animals, hazing them away from the house and towards the open Arkansas range land. Even as the horses' hooves drummed out loud in the night, from various points about the Dragoons' camp came more rebel yells, shots and flickering flames as hay and straw piles took fire. Disturbed horses snorted and moved restlessly, voices shouted questions, curses and orders, the whole punctuated by the wild ringing rebel war yells and occasional shots.

Up at the big house, the band came to a discordant halt in the middle of a Virginia reel. The more sober officers reacted first. Leaving their partners, they led the rush from the building. Outside all was pandemonium. A bugler sounded assembly, blowing lustily but without effect. Celebrating men poured from the sutler's building, most of them too drunk to make any logical deductions. The sound of shooting increased, yells went up as horses were freed from two company picket lines to add to the confusion.

One of the first people from the officers' mess was Colonel Verncombe, commanding the Dragoons. Halting, he stood glaring around him at the confusion. Fires blazed from three different points, men dashed about wildly and without any co-ordination while a flurry of revolver shots down by A Company's picket lines merged into the noise of stampeding horses.

"What the hell?" yelped a major, cannoning into his colonel.

"It's a full-scale attack!" Verncombe answered. "Get down and start organizing your—"

"Look there!" yelled a lieutenant, pointing to where flames licked up the walls of the officers' stables.

"Get men down to it!" Verncombe barked back. "Save our horses and gear if you can. Where the hell's the sergeant of the guard. Officer of the day! Find the guard. The rest of you, to your companies. On the double!"

"Can we help, Vic?" asked an infantry colonel, who, along with several of his officers, had been a guest at the ball.

"Keep the civilians and womenfolk inside and from under foot, Paul," Verncombe replied, watching his officers scatter to their companies.

Long before any defence could be organized the firing died down and the sound of hooves faded into the distance. Cursing non-coms restrained their excited men and prevented them wasting ammunition shooting at shadows. Sweating officers started to check on the damage inflicted by the raiders and asked questions with regard to the strength of the force which attacked them.

An hour later a glowering Verncombe watched his company commanders gathering around. Face almost black with controlled fury, he waited to hear their reports. A smoke-blackened lieutenant came first, after an abortive attempt to douse the fire at the officers' stables.

"We couldn't save anything, sir," he said. "But at least the rebels took all the horses out before firing it."

"That figures," grunted Verncombe. "How about the sentry?"

"We found him stretched out on the ground, clear of the building. Been struck from behind. I've sent him to the surgeon."

"Good. How about it, Major Klieg?"

"They destroyed our hay supply and the corn stored by Company C, sir," answered the major. "Cut the picket lines, but my men managed to drive them off before they could do more than scatter the horses. Horses ran back into the camp and I've a detail rounding them up."

"And casualties?" asked Verncombe.

"Not in my company, sir. I don't think we got any of them; or if we did, the rebs carried them off."

Other reports came in. Company A had lost all its horses and half of Company E's mounts had gone, while the rest scattered through the disturbed camp. Three fodder stacks were either burned out or so badly damaged that they would be of no use in feeding the regiment's horses. While there had been some stiff fighting, casualties proved to be light. A few slight wounds and no deaths came as a result of the raid, although various claims were made as to the number of the enemy killed.

"Sounds like an entire regiment jumped us," said Verncombe dryly as he listened to his company commanders' reports.

Naturally no soldier wanted to say a small force caused such havoc in his camp and so most of the claims would be exaggerated. Knowing this, Verncombe decided that a company—a well-trained and organized company—of Confederate cavalry had made the attack.

"Who do you reckon it was?" he asked the senior major.

"Texas Light Cavalry, sir," the other answered without any hesitation.

"That's Captain Dusty Fog's company, sir," another officer broke in. "One of my men claims to have seen him before. Said he couldn't miss knowing Fog. Great, big, bearded feller on a black stallion eighteen hands high if it's an inch. The soldier claims to have seen Fog leading one party and thinks he might have hit him."

"What's amusing you, Major Pearce?" growled Verncombe, glaring at the commander of Company D as that worthy let out a low guffaw of laughter.

"Remarkable feller that Captain Fog, sir," Pearce replied. "One of my sergeants claims that he saw Fog and helped drive him off before he could free our mounts. Says he's sure he put a .44 ball in Fog before the rebs pulled back."

"An attack like this would be typical Texas Light Cavalry work though, sir," one of the officers pointed out.

"They've never struck in this area," another objected.

"A thing like that wouldn't worry Fog," Verncombe put in.

Over the past year the name of Captain Dusty Fog, Texas Light Cavalry, had risen to almost legendary heights. To the Union troops in Arkansas the name meant more than that of the South's other two top raiders, John Singleton Mosby and Turner Ashby. At the head of a company of hard-riding Texans, Dusty Fog struck like a tornado, coming unexpectedly and creating havoc, then disappearing again. His men could out-ride and out-shoot any Union outfit; although no Yankee cared to even think it, much less admit such an unpalatable fact.

A raid of the kind which just struck the Dragoons would be typical Dusty Fog tactics. Yet Verncombe wondered about certain aspects of the attack. The stunning of the stable guard and the freeing of the officers' horses did not strike him as being unusual. Dusty Fog fought in a chivalrous manner and would not kill unless in battle, if he could avoid doing so. Nor would he leave horses to burn, especially good quality mounts his own side could use against the Yankees. No, those two points did not worry Verncombe. The colonel felt surprised at the minor, comparatively speaking, damage inflicted on his surprised and disrupted camp. Under such conditions, he might have expected far greater losses of horses at least.

Suddenly a chilling thought struck Verncombe, one that drove all others from his head. One of his companies was at that moment acting as escort to a visiting general, taking him to Fort Smith in the Indian Nations. Grabbing senior Union officers and whisking them off behind the Confederate lines had long been a prime activity of Dixie's raiding trio. If Dusty Fog should hear of the general he might easily strike in that direction.

On giving the matter further thought, Verncombe decided his fears were unfounded. The route taken by the general lay to the north of Russelville. With such useful booty as almost a hundred head of prime horses in his hands, Dusty Fog would be highly unlikely to go further north. In Fog's place, Verncombe knew he would head straight back towards the Ouachita River and the safety of Confederate-held territory.

"Best get back to the guests some of you," he told his officers. "The rest start getting things cleared up."

"Do we take after them, sir?" asked the commander of Company A, seething with rage at the loss of all his horses.

"By the time we could, they'll have too much of a head start," Verncombe replied bitterly. "All right. Let's make a start."

The ball had come to an end, but the infantry colonel succeeded in keeping the civilian guests from bothering the hard-pressed Dragoons. After a time, the visitors began to prepare to leave.

In the confusion following the attack, nobody missed a very beautiful blonde girl who had been present earlier in the evening. The Dragoon officers had too much on their minds to pay much attention to their departing guests. If either the infantry officers or the civilians missed the girl, they said nothing, thinking she was a member of a Dragoon family. During the evening, she had mingled with the other people present; pleasant, witty and yet never staying with one group for any length of time, so nobody missed her. However, it was an indisputable fact that she neither went with the Dragoon families to their quarters, nor left with the other guests.

## CHAPTER TWO

## Miss Boyd In Distress

A mile from the Dragoons' camp, the girl slowed her two horses and allowed the officers' mounts she had driven before her to stream off into the night. Twisting around in her saddle, she looked back to where flickering fires and some noise marked the camp's site. By now the shooting had died down, but she could guess at the confusion it caused among the Dragoons.

After ensuring that she was not being followed, the girl started her horses moving once more. She rode through the darkness for a short time until coming to the bank of a small stream. Turning her mounts downstream, she continued along its bank until reaching a wagon road and ford. There she went into some bushes, slipped from the saddle and let the horses graze.

Time passed and hooves drummed as a rider came down the road. Instantly the girl drew her Dance, cocking it and handling it in a manner which showed she knew how to use it. Moving to her horses' heads, she peered through the bushes to where a rider approached. The darkness prevented her from being able to identify the approaching man, or even tell if he be civilian or soldier. Hefting her Dance with the right hand and gripping the bay's reins with her left, the girl began to whistle a tune. At the first sound, the rider's hand dropped hipwards and lifted holding a gun.

"Southrons, hear your country call you," he said in a low voice.

"Up, lest worse than death befall you," answered the girl, holstering her Dance in the certainty that the other be friend.

The whistling of "Dixie" might have been done by a Yankee, but the rider knew few Union supporters would know the fiercely patriotic words put by General Albert Miles to Daniel D. Emmet's tune. So he holstered his gun and rode closer.

"How did it go?" asked the girl, coming from cover.

"Smooth as a snake's belly, Miss Boyd," the man replied.

"Were any of your men hurt?"

"Nary a one. We did just like you said, moved in and waited. The Yankees were all whopping it up, or in their beds. Didn't hardly see as much as a sentry. Got away with a fair bunch of hosses. What'll we do with 'em?"

"Send them west. If you meet a Confederate Army outfit hand them over. If not push them into the Indian Nations."

Either way the horses would be lost to the Yankees for no Indian would return a bunch of prime horses to the Union Army.

"You sure planned things slick, Miss Boyd," enthused the man. "Me and the boys didn't fire more than a dozen shots at most. Those Yankees made up for it. Did any of 'em shoot each other?"

"It's possible," Belle Boyd agreed. "Say, I had to destroy those maid's clothes you brought to me."

"That's all right, ma'am," the man replied. "Can we do anything more for you-all?"

"No. Scatter to your homes like you usually do, after you've got rid of the horses. And thanks for your help."

"It's been a real pleasure, ma'am," answered the man, watching the girl mount the bay and ride off leading the roan. He gave an admiring grin and rubbed the neck of his horse. "Yes, sir, hoss. That Belle Boyd's sure some gal. Wonder what brought her out this ways."

Holding her horse at a steady, mile-eating trot, Belle Boyd rode south-east along the trail. While the man she had just left, and his band of Southern patriots, had proved to be of the greatest help to her, she knew that she must have the aid of a larger, better armed force to make use of the information gathered since her return from Europe. A dozen men, no matter how brave or loyal, could not handle the next part in Belle's plan. On the next occasion Belle organized a raid on a Union force, she wanted to really have a strong Confederate Army outfit at her back.

All she had to do was ride across about sixty miles of hostile territory, ford the Ouachita without being caught, and report to the nearest Confederate force to be granted the aid she needed. That her request would receive immediate attention she did not for a moment doubt, for Belle possessed an almost legendary fame among the grey-clad soldiers of the South.

Born into a rich Southern family, Belle grew up with every advantage and luxury, yet had a restless spirit which prevented her from becoming a pampered milk-sop. As a child she always preferred boys' games to girlish pastimes and her indulgent father, who wanted a son, taught her to ride, shoot and other male accomplishments. Nor did she ever forget them, and continued to defy conventions through her teens. The clouds of strife grew in the South and Belle's father had been an outspoken champion of every sovereign state's right to secede from the Union if its policies and interests came into conflict with the remainder —one of the main causes of the Civil War, although the Union supporters used the slavery issue as being more suited to induce their people to fight.

One night, shortly before the start of the War, a bunch of Union supporters attacked Belle's home. Belle's mother and father were killed in the attack and the girl received a wound, being helped to escape by some of her family's "down-trodden and abused" slaves. By the time Belle recovered from her wound, the War had started, and she put her newly-developed hatred of the Yankees to good use by becoming a spy. Without formal training, Belle still became a very useful agent for the Confederacy. She gathered and passed on information, often delivering her own messages instead of relying on a courier. Old Stonewall Jackson himself often referred to Belle as his best courier and admitted that she and the South's other lady spy, Rose Greenhow—Rose gathering the information and Belle delivering it—made the defeat of the Yankees at the first battle of Bull Run possible.

With such a solid recommendation as that at her back, Belle knew she could rely upon the aid of the Confederate troops in Arkansas, once she found them.

Keeping upon a steady seven-miles-an-hour trot, and changing horses frequently, Belle followed the trail to the southeast. One talent developed since the start of the War, an invaluable one in her chosen line of work, was the ability to carry the memory of a map in her head. Thinking on what she had seen at the Dragoons' camp, while searching Colonel Verncombe's office for the information she required, Belle knew that she must cross the Coon Fork of the Arkansas River. Her discussion with the Southern patriots warned her that the Coon Fork ran fast and deep for many miles and could only be crossed by a bridge—and every bridge carried a strong Union guard. With that knowledge in mind, Belle continued to follow the trail and lay her plans for crossing the river when she reached it.

Dawn began to creep up, faint but ever-growing grey forcing out the blackness of the eastern sky. Halting her horses, Belle slipped from the saddle and looked around her. Not a half-mile ahead, although still hidden from sight, lay the Coon Fork, and the trail she followed crossed the river over a bridge.

Opening one of her travelling bags, which hung strapped to the bay's saddle, Belle took out a carefully folded white satin ball gown. The gown, made to her own design, had been much admired at the Dragoons' camp and packed when Belle changed ready for departure. Two other boxes lay in the bag, one containing her blonde, red and black wigs, all so carefully made that only a *very* close inspection could differentiate between them and a real head of hair when Belle wore one or the other. The second box carried a dark blue Union officers' fatigue cap with gold braid decorating it. Taking out the cap, Belle donned it at a rakish angle which served to partially hide her face under the peak's shadow. She repacked and secured the bag and then unstrapped the overcoat which hung militarily neat on the cantle of the roan's saddle.

Although the "cloak coat" proved to be somewhat large, Belle found no difficulty in donning it or fastening the frog buttons to keep it in place. She decided to leave the sleeve length cloak in position as it helped to further disguise her shape. Having used a similar bluff on more than one occasion, Belle felt no great anxiety as she mounted the roan, gripped the bay's reins in her left hand, and started to ride towards the bridge.

Despite her cool appearance, Belle felt a momentary twinge of doubt and concern as she came into sight of the bridge. Fear of Confederate raids led the Union forces to maintain a strong guard on every important bridge, and the nature of the Coon's flow made it imperative that the bridge she approached stayed in use. So a force of almost company strength had been camped by the bridge.

Belle based her arrival on coming in with the dawn, at a

time when human energy was at its lowest ebb. From the look of the lines of pup tents and lack of burning fires, most of the guard detail lay in their blankets. No crew manned the squat, evil-looking Vandenburg Volley gun which covered the further approaches to the bridge, but she did not doubt that its crew slept in the pup tent close by it, or that it stood with all eighty-five .50 calibre barrels loaded ready to discharge at any hostile force foolish enough to try to rush from the other side of the river.

Only one sentry stood watch, leaning against the upright support of the bridge and, from all appearances, not more than half asleep. However, a disturbing sight to Belle's eyes were the half dozen or so men saddling their horses beyond the line of tents.

Sucking in a breath, Belle continued to ride, apparently unconcerned, down the trail towards the bridge. Hearing the hoof-beats, the sentry turned his attention towards the approaching figure. He studied the two fine-looking horses and could identify an officer's fatigue cap and overcoat. Having seen numerous officers cross the bridge, the sentry regarded the approaching rider with no great concern nor suspicion.

In addition to possessing a naturally husky contralto voice, Belle was a good mimic. Approaching the sentry, she slowed down her horse. By keeping her head down, she prevented him from making out too much of her features as she growled, "Lieutenant Murray, 6th New Jersey Dragoons, riding dispatch."

A formal enough announcement and one the soldier might have taken at its face value. However, the man was an old soldier, the kind who took his duty seriously and stayed alert even after a long spell on his post. His eyes took in the two horses, noting their excellent condition and breeding. Such animals would belong to an officer and attracted no suspicion. Then his gaze ran up the booted legs. The cloak-coat trailed down far enough to hide Belle's breeches and her boots gave no sign of anything being

wrong. Nor did the cloak-coat—until the man's eyes
reached the cuffs of the sleeves. For a moment he studied
the decorative knot formed by three silk braids and suspicion clicked in his head. The rider claimed to be a lieutenant in the Dragoons, yet those triple braids announced the
wearer held rank as major.

One did not spend twenty years in the Army without
learning caution when handling officers. There were a
number of explanations, most of them innocent, why a
shavetail should be wearing a major's cloak-coat.

"Do you have anything to identify yourself, mis—" he
began, looking up at Belle as he moved closer. The words
trailed off as he realized that the face did not belong to a
man. "Who the   "

Jerking her foot from the stirrup iron, Belle delivered a
stamping kick full into the sentry's face. The impact rocked
the man backwards, sending him stumbling clear of the
horse. Involuntarily his finger closed on the trigger of his
Springfield carbine and the gun crashed as he fell over
backwards.

Even as the man reeled away from her, Belle set the two
horses running across the bridge. Behind her, she heard
yells and knew the shot had roused the camp. A glance to
one side showed her the group of men at the horse lines
were hurriedly completing their saddling and would very
soon be giving pursuit. Mounted on fresh horses against
her own which had been working all night, the men would
give her a hard run for her money.

At which point Belle remembered the Vandenburg gun
and realized the deadly menace it posed to her life as she
raced her horse across the bridge. Already the more capable members of its crew had left their tent and hurled
themselves towards their cumbersome but deadly weapon.
Cumbersome it might be, but Belle knew its full potential
under the present conditions and doing the work for which
it had been designed. The Vandenburg could be likened to
a shotgun in that all its bullets left the barrels at the same

moment, fired by a central charge. In a test, a 191-barrel model Vandenburg put ninety per cent of its balls into a six-foot square at one hundred yards and Belle doubted if the smaller type behind her would prove any less accurate. The eighty-five bullets would sweep the bridge like a death-dealing broom; nothing on the wooden confines could escape them.

Although freshly wakened from sleep, the gunner reached his weapon with commendable speed. Throwing himself to the firing position, he took aim through the square, three-inch aperture of the rear sight. Specially designed to cover the spread of the bullets, the sight showed him the speeding rider had almost reached the end of the bridge. While being a fine weapon for defending a restricted area such as a bridge, the gun possessed one serious disadvantage. It took time to unscrew and open the breech, reload the eighty-five separate chambers of the barrels, replace the central charge and percussion cap, then close and lock the breech into place again. If the gun missed its mark, the escaping rider would be well out of range long before another discharge could be fired.

Expecting at any moment to feel the crashing impact of the Vandenburg's volley tear into her, Belle watched the end of the bridge rushing closer. She started to turn the roan, drawing the bay after her and blessing it for being so obedient to control that it followed without fuss. She felt the end post of the bridge brush her leg in passing and the bay drew slightly forward on its loaded roan companion. Each racing stride carried her closer and closer to being beyond the area of the Vandenburg's spreading charge and still the gun did not fire.

Then it came, a roaring bellow that shattered the dawn, drowning out every other noise. The gun bucked and slammed back hard with its terrible recoil and its volley of lead hissed forth along the bridge. Even as he fired, the gunner realized he had left things a shade too late to catch the rider in the centre of the bullets' pattern. Maybe too late for a hit even.

Belle heard the "splat!" of a close-passing bullet splitting the air by her head. Then there came a soggy thud, a jarring sensation just behind her leg. The roan screamed, lurched and started to go down, caught by a chance ball after the main charge missed by inches.

Charging through the disturbed camp, the six-man detail, who had been preparing to ride escort on a supply wagon to their regiment's camp, let out wild yells of triumph as they saw the roan going down. They had been unable to cross the bridge until the Vandenburg bellowed, but now could do so and pick up the rider. Or so they believed. Almost as soon as the gun fired, the leading riders reached the end of the bridge. Startled by the noise and flame, one of the horses shied violently, throwing its rider before stampeding wildly. The remaining four men, a sergeant and three privates, managed to keep control of their mounts and headed across the bridge at a gallop.

Feeling the roan going down, Belle kicked her feet from the stirrups. She clung on to the bay's reins, swinging the horse round as it tried to run on. Praying that the bay's bit and bridle held firm, Belle kicked her left leg over the roan's saddle and jumped clear. From the moment her feet touched the ground, she started to run, fighting desperately to keep her balance. A wild grab closed her fingers on the bay's saddle, gripping the pommel and clinging on desperately. The bay slid on its haunches as it tried to obey the orders of its reins. In doing so, it presented Belle with a chance to get a foot in the stirrup. Hampered by the cloak-coat, Belle could not make a flying mount. In fact she found difficulty in swinging herself afork the bay at all. After a momentary pause, the bay started moving again, going along the trail at a run. Belle's free foot stamped down once and she clung to the saddle grimly. With a desperate heave, she managed to raise herself, throw a leg across the saddle and dig a toe into the security of the stirrup iron to keep herself astride the bay. Doing so cost her valuable time which she could not spare.

Better mounted than the others, the sergeant drew ahead during the dash over the bridge. On reaching the other side, he charged after the fleeing girl and drew his Colt to fire a shot. On hearing the bullet hiss by her head, Belle glanced back and saw her danger. A keen judge of horseflesh, she knew the sergeant's mount ought to be able to run down the bay, being more fresh than the animal Belle sat upon. That shot had been mighty lucky to come so close when fired from the unstable platform offered by a racing horse. Lucky maybe, but Belle knew a lucky shot killed just as dead as one taken with the most careful aim.

Belle knew she must do something to prevent the sergeant drawing any nearer. Remembering how the overcoat impeded her, Belle saw a way. Keeping the bay running at a slow gallop, Belle started to wriggle from the coat. In this the garment's extra size proved advantageous. Unhooking the frog buttons, Belle freed the coat and, working carefully, wriggled her arms from the sleeves. The left arm came free as another shot narrowly missed her. Grabbing down, she caught the reins in her left hand and jerked the right out of the sleeve. Instantly the coat whisked behind her.

Too late the sergeant saw his danger. Dropping his Colt, he tried to check his horse's forward rush as the coat came fluttering down before him. The coat struck the horse's forelegs, tangling them and bringing the animal crashing down. Pitching over the horse's head, the sergeant tried to break his fall. He was only partially successful, landing rolling but breaking his shoulder. Ignoring their fallen noncom, the remainder of the party charged on after the fleeing girl.

Having ridden since early childhood, Belle knew the dangers of galloping a horse over a hard-packed surface like the trail. Due to the jarring impact on the iron-hard earth, the hooves or legs might easily be damaged, in which case Belle would fall a victim to the pursuing Yankees. Another point she considered was that she stood a better chance of escape while riding over rough ground, being willing to gamble her skill on a horse against that of the following soldiers.

Turning the horse, she headed it from the trail and out across the rolling country. Underfoot the springy grass and loose soil served as a cushion for the racing hooves and lessened the danger of injury. Belle used all her skill to ease the horse's task in what she knew must be a long, hard race for freedom. Had the bay been fresh, she could ride the soldiers out of sight in a couple of miles. With it tired from a long journey, she knew she must aid it all she could.

Throwing her weight forward to be taken on the knees and stirrups, Belle lifted herself clear of the seat of the saddle and bent forward at the waist. Riding in that fashion offered as little interference as possible to the thrust and stride of the bay's hind legs and acted as an aid to speed. To increase her control and give a better feel of the horse's mouth, Belle took a shorter grip on the reins. Her whole arms gave to the movements of the horse's head, but she maintained her control over the animal. Under such conditions a horse's natural instinct for self-preservation tended to make it rush wildly along, so Belle knew the need for control.

Behind her one of the men did not understand the danger. His horse careered along, its reins flapping. Losing his hat, the soldier panicked and had no idea of collecting, regaining control of the racing animal. He drew ahead of the others, but found the horse running off to one side at an angle which grew more acute to the direction of his quarry. Grabbing a firm hold of the reins, the soldier tried to correct this. Feeling the savage tug at its mouth, the horse tried to fight against the pressure, lost its footing and went down. The rider went flying, struck the ground and scraped along in the dirt before coming to a moaning, barely conscious halt.

Not knowing that her pursuers now numbered only three, Belle kept her horse running. Luck more than good horsemanship kept the remainder of the Yankees in their saddles and their fresher horses lost no ground. On they went and a mile fell behind them. Sliding down slopes in a rump-scraping churning of dust and flying stones, fighting upwards when necessary, tearing along level ground, the bay ran like a creature possessed. Belle gave up her entire attention to controlling and handling the horse, never daring to relax for a moment. Sweat poured down her face, trickling into and stinging her eyes.

Ahead lay a slope, steeper and higher than any other so far climbed. Under Belle, the bay showed signs of distress. She estimated they had now covered almost two miles from the bridge. If the bay made it to the top of the slope, she stood a chance of escaping. By that time the Yankees' horses must be almost as leg-weary as her own mount. Glances taken to the rear during the chase had told her of the following men's abilities and she knew their horses must be suffering. The slope ought to prove their breaking point.

Through the sweat-mist in her eyes Belle saw shapes on the slope above her. A trio of riders appeared on the top and started down. Though blurred, her eyes still picked out enough to tell that the men wore uniforms.

Desperately she tried to turn the horse. It staggered, lost its footing and came to a churning halt. Belle gave a groan as her hand dropped towards the butt of her Dance. This area lay well within the sphere of Union control and the men above her cut off her escape. It seemed that Belle's mission would come to a sudden end.

## CHAPTER THREE

## Miss Boyd Makes Her Point

"Kiowa's wig-wagging, Cousin Dusty."

Almost before Lieutenant Red Blaze finished speaking, Captain Dustine Edward Marsden Fog raised his right hand in a signal which brought Company C's V-shaped formation to a halt. The tanned, grey-clad riders sat on their horses like statues, making no chatter as they scanned the range around them or looked ahead to where their outfit's forward scout stood by his mount looking in their direction and signalling to the column.

How close did the Dragoon's description fit the man who had carved himself such a name throughout the war-torn country?

The black stallion between Dusty Fog's knees stood only seventeen hands high, but a matter of four inches could be overlooked. However, Dusty could hardly be described as a great, big feller when he stood a mere five feet six inches in his Jefferson boots. Not that he was puny with the small size. His shoulders had width that hinted at strength, he tapered down to a lean, fighting man's middle, with straight, powerful legs. A white Jeff Davis hat rode his dusty blond hair, its broad brim offering shade for his tanned, intelligent, handsome young face. Cut of good quality material, the uniform he wore emphasized his physique although it did not entirely conform with the Confederate States Army's *Manual of Dress Regulations*. True the stand-up collar bore the required triple three-inch long, half-inch wide gold braid bars of his rank, but he did not wear the black cravat at his throat. Instead a scarlet silk bandana, tightly rolled and knotted, trailed its long ends down over the cadet-grey of the jacket. While the double row of buttons, seven to the row, ran up his double-breasted jacket and its sleeves bore the double strand gold braid decoration of a captain, it lacked the skirt "extending half-way between hip and knee" expected by a strict adherent to regulations. His tight-legged breeches conformed to regulations, the yellow cavalry stripe running down the outer seam. His weapon belt did not conform, for instead of a single revolver in a close-topped holster and a sabre, the wide brown belt, worn lower than normal military fashion, supported a matched brace of bone-handled 1860 Army Colts butt forward in open-topped holsters. Not that Dusty ignored the *arme blanche* of the true cavalryman. He sat in a range saddle, low of horn and with double cinches; a long Manila rope strapped to one side of the horn, and at the other hung a Haiman Brothers sabre, made to his own specifications by one of the finest companies in the world.

The Yankee Dragoon did not come very close in his description of Dusty Fog. Not a great, big, black-bearded feller, but a youngster of eighteen—yet one full grown in the arts of war.

"Hold up the company, Cousin Red," he ordered. "Let's go, Billy Jack."

Red Blaze, a pugnaciously handsome, freckle-faced youngster with a fiery thatch of hair that showed from under his pushed-back hat, nodded. Dressed in a similar

manner to his illustrious cousin, he topped Dusty by a good
six inches and had a powerful frame. Yet he never gave a
thought to his superior size when Dusty gave him an order.
Like most people, maybe more so as he grew up with
Dusty, Red never thought of the other in mere feet and
inches. To the admiring Red, that small Texan stood the
tallest of them all and he felt no envy or jealousy at his
cousin's fame.

Tall, gangling, his mournful-featured face and prominent Adam's apple giving him a hang-dog, care-worn appearance, Sergeant-major Billy Jack followed his captain
as the other rode towards the lead-scout.

Despite the strangulation of the Union blockade upon
Confederate ports, the men under Dusty's command all appeared to be well mounted, dressed and armed. They relied
upon the Yankee army for most of the necessities of life,
raiding to replenish their supply of arms, powder and lead,
or whatever commodity happened to be needed. Although
few of them had heard of it, they were by birth, upbringing
and training, ideally suited to follow the Napoleonic way
of making war support war.

Organized and financed by rich men of the Lone Star
State, the Texas Light Cavalry was commanded by officers
who knew the rudiments and refinements of horseback
fighting through much personal experience against expo-
nents of the art such as Mexican *banditos* and *Coman-
cheros* or the various hostile Indian tribes who roamed their
State's vast area. Every man in the regiment had been
reared with a horse as a means of survival instead of a mere
method of transport. Skilled almost from teeth-cutting days
in the use of firearms, they came to war with at least as
much experience as a regular Union Army outfit and far
more than any of the volunteer regiments the Yankees used
to maintain their hold on the north-east land beyond the
Arkansas River.

Kiowa, a tall, lean, Indian-dark man in the uniform of a
sergeant, had halted his horse back from the edge of a

slope and stood looking down. While nobody, except possibly his mother, would call him handsome, he possessed all the keen senses and knowledge of an Indian brave-heart warrior and made an ideal scout upon whom Dusty never failed to trust the safety of the company.

"Yankees chasing a gal," Kiowa remarked, an unusually long speech for him.

Which, while not gabby, explained everything happening below. Moving forward cautiously, Dusty and Billy Jack looked down the slope and witnessed the final stages of the chase. They saw Belle Boyd start her lathered, leg-weary horse on the difficult climb up the slope.

"She'll not make it," Dusty remarked. "Let's go help her."

Returning to their waiting horses, the three men made rapid mounts and urged the animals down the slope. All showed their considerable riding skill in staying afork their horses on ground most people would either have ignored or walked down. Seeing the girl look up, Dusty expected her to make further efforts to reach them. Instead she reined the horse in a turn and only succeeded in bringing it to a sliding halt. Her right hand went down and drew the revolver she wore. Guessing that sweat blinded her, or at least prevented her from recognizing the cadet-grey of his uniform, Dusty let out a ringing rebel yell.

Never had any sound come so sweetly to Belle's ears than did that wild "Yeah!" Dusty let forth. Two shots crackled from below, but the bullets went wild. Having ridden hard, fast and far, the Yankee soldiers were in no shape for fancy revolver shooting. Apparently they realized that and saw their danger, for they turned their leg-weary horses and started to gallop back towards the safety of the Coon Fork bridge.

"Take after them!" Dusty ordered. "We don't want them stirring up the whole damned country."

"Yo!" answered Billy Jack, throwing an admiring

glance at the girl as he and Kiowa passed her in their reckless ride down the slope.

Belle thrust away her Dance and gave her full attention to regaining control of her horse. With that done, she raised a hand to rub the sweat from her eyes. Being in good physical condition, the girl soon had her breath back and could think clearly once more. Studying Dusty, she reached rapid, and correct, conclusions. The uniform told her some of it, but not quite as much as the insignia on his hat. One did not need to be a student of military matters to recognize that silver star in a circle as the badge of the Texas Light Cavalry.

From Dusty, the girl turned her attention to where Billy Jack and Kiowa had reached the foot of the slope and now urged their horses after the the fleeing Yankees.

"Can your men handle it?" she asked.

"Unless there's a whole lot more Yankees close up they can," Dusty replied.

"The nearest are almost two miles off."

"Then the boys'll have caught up with those three before they reach help."

Watching the expert manner in which the two Texans handled their racing horses, Belle could understand her rescuer's quiet confidence. Even mounted on fresh animals, the Yankees would be hard put to out-ride the pursuing Texans. She turned her eyes to Dusty.

"I suppose you are wondering who I am and why the Yankees were after me."

"The thought had hit me," Dusty admitted.

"May I ask who you are, sir?"

"The name's Fog."

Belle glanced at Dusty's collar bars and then looked him over. Being a shrewd judge of human nature, she saw beyond his youth and small size to the real man underneath. However, it did take some believing that he really was—

"Captain *Dusty* Fog?"

"I've been called that at times."

Shots sounded from the foot of the slope and ended any more conversation for a few moments. Turning, Belle and Dusty looked down to see how the two non-coms fared against the trio of Yankees. It seemed that the Texans had managed pretty well. Even as Belle looked down, she saw one of the blue-clad soldiers slide sideways from his horse and crash to the ground. By all appearances the Yankees decided flight would not save them and turned to make a fight. Fighting offered them little better chance when matched by a couple of highly skilled horse-back warriors like Kiowa and Billy Jack. When the second soldier took lead in his shoulders, the third decided to yell "calf rope" and surrender. Throwing aside his revolver, he jerked his arms into the air—just in time to stop Kiowa cutting him down.

"They didn't get far," Belle remarked.

"I never figured they would," Dusty replied. "Let's get back to my company."

Although Belle could hardly hide her delight at learning that the fates threw her in with the very aid she needed, she managed to conceal her emotions. "What will you do with the Yankees?" she asked as they turned their horses up the slope.

"Take them with us until we get where we're going."

"May I ask where that would be?"

A smile flickered on Dusty's face. "May *I* ask what you said your name was?" he countered.

"Would you believe me if I told you that I'm Belle Boyd?"

"A Southern gentleman never doubts a lady's word, ma'am," Dusty replied, "but I'm a soldier—and they like proof."

"When we get to your company, I'll give you proof," Belle promised.

On reaching the company, Belle found that she would

not be given an immediate chance to prove her identity.
Dusty showed a commendable reluctance to staying out in
such an exposed position and prepared to move on. Although he could see his cousin seething with unasked questions, Dusty let Red stew for a time.

"We'll be making a long halt at the foot of the slope,
ma'am," Dusty told the girl. "I reckon your horse'll make
it that far. When we move on, you can use one of our
reserve horses—if you can handle it."

"If it has hair and the usual number of legs on each
corner, I can handle it," Belle answered.

Although Belle's arrival and appearance caused something of a stir among the soldiers, discipline remained and
they kept their comments down to low mutters while moving off. Belle had long since stopped feeling embarrassed
at the attention her revealing riding clothes attracted among
members of both sexes.

At the foot of the slope Billy Jack and Kiowa stood by
their horses and guarded two dejected prisoners, one tend-
ing to the other's shoulder. A still, blue-uniformed shape
sprawled on the ground beyond them.

"Had to kill that one, Cap'n Dusty," Billy Jack reported.

"It happens," Dusty replied. "Take a point, Kiowa.
We'll make our long halt by that stream down there."

"Yo!" Kiowa answered, going to his horse.

During her dash for freedom Belle had barely noticed
the small stream. Surrounded by a force of skilled fighting
men, she could allow her tired horse to drink in safety. She
noticed that the two prisoners were in no way mistreated,
but that an escort surrounded them and prevented any
chance of escape.

Much as Belle wanted to lay her suggestions before
Dusty, she set about attending to her horse first. To fail in
such an elementary precaution was foreign to her nature,
and she knew failure would lower her standing in Dusty's
eyes. While stripping off the bay's saddle, she felt Dusty's
eyes on her. Belle Boyd had a reputation for being real

good with horses and she had to prove it to an acknowledged master in that line.

After the bay had drunk its fill and indulged in a good roll, Belle accepted the loan of a feed bag from one of the Texans, collected some grain from the supply carried on a pack horse and fed her mount. All around her men carried out the same tasks, working with the minimum of supervision. Not until every horse had been cared for did the men prepare their own meal. Nor did the Texans relax and grow careless. On each side, far from the column but in sight of it, keen-eyed pickets kept watch for any sign of the enemy.

Opening one of her bags, Belle took out a pair of black silk stockings. She slipped a hand into the top of one and drew a slip of paper from where it had been concealed in a pocket carefully and cunningly built into the upper section. Handing the paper to Dusty, she watched him open and read it.

"It is genuine," she remarked.

"I know old Stonewall's signature. Nobody else could write that bad," Dusty replied, looking again at the message identifying Belle Boyd and requesting all C.S.A. personnel to render her every assistance. "You'd get this from Colonel Cope in Atlanta, I reckon."

"There's no Colonel Cope in our Secret Service," Belle answered, pleased that the other did not take the document entirely for granted. "I don't often have orders but when I do, I get them from General Mandeville."

"Pleased to meet you, Miss Boyd," Dusty smiled. "May I present my second-in-command, Mr. Blaze. Red, meet Miss Belle Boyd."

"Right pleased to know you, ma'am," Red greeted.

"My pleasure, sir," she replied. "Now may I ask what you're doing here, Captain Fog?"

"General Hardin sent me up this way to create a diversion. Stir up the Yankees and draw some of their men out this way. He's sending Company A in to destroy a Union supply depot near Little Rock. I figured on wrecking a bridge up there on the Coon Fork of the Arkansas."

"That's where I came from and picked up my escort," Belle warned. "There's a company and a Vandenburg volley gun guarding it."

"We figured on at least that much," Red put in. "Dusty's taken better guarded things than that."

"Would you be interested in hitting at an even more important target?" Belle inquired, smiling a little at Red's open admiration for his smaller cousin.

"If it's worthwhile," Dusty agreed.

"Would you say raiding a U.S. Army paymaster with fifty thousand dollars in gold is worthwhile?" asked the girl.

Dusty and Red exchanged glances and Belle could see she had their interest.

"I can think of less important things," Dusty finally said. "Let's hear about it, Miss Boyd."

"It began after I returned from Europe a few days back," Belle explained. "I went to Washington and picked up some information from one of our agents. The U.S. Government is sending fifty thousand dollars in gold to the Indian Nations. It's partly payment for troops there and the rest to be divided among the chiefs of the Osage, Pawnee, Cow and Arikara tribes as an inducement for them to keep the peace and resist the suggestions of the Cherokee Nation to take sides in the War. So I came straight out here and finished at the Dragoons' camp near Russelville. I learned all I could, then headed for our territory. It would have been tight if I'd had to cross the Ouachita and find a Confederate outfit, but meeting you here gives us plenty of time. I know the route they'll take with the shipment and the other details."

"How big an escort will it have?" asked Dusty.

"The Yankees don't want to attract too much attention to the shipment for obvious reasons. So ostensibly it will be merely guarding the carriage of a general on a tour of inspection. The escort will consist, in this area, of a large company of Dragoons, between fifty and sixty men."

"A fair number," Dusty remarked, thinking that his force numbered only forty and that at least six of them would be needed to guard the reserve and pack horses.

"Only Dragoons though," grinned Red, his eyes glinting with the light of battle. "Comes to a fight, we've damned nigh got that many outnumbered."

"That depends," Dusty drawled, eyeing his impetuous cousin tolerantly.

"On what?" asked Belle.

"Whether we take them on under our terms and on our ground, or theirs," Dusty answered. "Tell me about your activities. Everything you've done since you came out here."

Speaking concisely and leaving out only the names of her helpers, a precaution Dusty admired, Belle gave the Texans a clear picture of everything she had done including her escape and how she covered her tracks.

"I'm sure nobody missed me in the excitement. And I reckon the sentry will insist he doesn't know who hit him," she concluded—which proved to be correct, for at that moment Private Hooley stood before his colonel and stoutly affirmed how he had been struck from behind by a person or persons unknown—"And if I know soldiers, they'll none of them be willing to admit they don't know how few men jumped them. In fact, I'd take money that they swear to seeing a Confederate company, probably your own, Captain Fog, jump them."

Dusty accepted the tribute to his face without any comment, being more concerned with the practical side of the matter. "Then the Dragoons may be out looking for us, he pointed out.

"It's possible," admitted Belle. "However, I'd guess that Colonel Verncombe won't bother. He'll believe that, having over fifty of his horses, you'll have made a fast run for the Ouachita, and will get right to clearing up the damage rather than waste time."

"Only thing to do is find out where the Yankee general

will be travelling then," Dusty commented and walked to
where his saddle lay on its side. Opening one of the
pouches, he took out a folded map and returned to the
others. Spreading the map Dusty looked at the girl. "Any
suggestions, ma'am?"

"You might try calling me 'Belle,' 'ma'am' makes me
feel old," she smiled. "They'll be going over the Crossland
Trace."

Examining the map, Dusty ran his finger along a line
marking the Crossland Trace, a wagon route running to the
north of Russelville and communicating with the Indian
Nations' forts. The map, looted from a Union Army camp,
was good and carried enough detail for Dusty to be able to
visualize the land through which the shipment travelled.
For almost five minutes he sat studying the map, while Red
and Belle left him to his thoughts. At last he looked at the
other two.

"How long before the shipment comes through?" he
asked.

"I'll send a man to relieve Kiowa," Red remarked, and
rose to give the order.

"Red appears to know you," Belle said and then answered Dusty's question. "Captain Christie met it this
morning and will be started out now. I'd say that we might
pick it up the day after tomorrow. An escort and carriage
won't be travelling at any speed."

"Reckon it won't," agreed Dusty. "All non-coms, Mr.
Blaze."

Knowing his cousin, as Belle said, Red had already
given the order which brought the company's sergeants and
corporals gathering about their leader. Dusty told them
their mission and eager rumbles went up among the half-
circle of tanned, tough-looking men. Then he proceeded to
explain his plan in detail, after scraping clear a piece of
earth on which to draw a large-scale map.

Belle watched everything and her original relief at being
rescued by Dusty grew to delight at her good fortune. Al-

ready she had made an estimation of Dusty's capabilities and knew her judgment was correct. Not only was the small Texan a top-grade fighting man, but he also possessed a shrewd, calculating brain—and used it. If attention to detail guaranteed success, then their mission must be a success. However, Dusty's plan surprised her in one respect and, when he finished talking, she brought up the point.

"I thought you might make your move further west."

"And I would," agreed Dusty, "if I could find a place so well suited to my idea. You'll stay with the reserve mounts' detail when we make our attack, Belle."

"With your permission, I'd rather go with your party," she objected.

"You, ma'am," grinned a burly corporal. "It'll be no place for a woman."

Sighing resignedly, Belle came to her feet in a swift, graceful move and faced the man, but looked towards Dusty. "I have this trouble every time," she remarked. "Well, it may as well be now as later."

"You've left me behind, Belle," Dusty answered.

"Every time I offer to take a hand in a fight, some big, strong man decides that it's no place for a woman and I have to prove my point," she explained, taking out her Dance and removing the percussion caps from its chamber. "Unload your gun, Corporal."

After glancing to Dusty for permission, and receiving it, the grinning corporal followed Belle's lead in rendering his right side Colt safe. Holstering his gun, he faced the girl from a distance of about four feet. Belle's right hand lifted to hover over the butt of her Dance.

Watching the girl, Dusty smiled a little, although his gaze directed at her feet instead of her hand. Instead of the normal stance for drawing and shooting, Belle's feet formed a T position about her shoulders' width apart, the left pointed at the corporal, the right's heel aimed at the centre of the left, and both knees slightly bent.

Down stabbed the corporal's hand in a smooth, fast move, fingers closing on and lifting the Colt. Even as his gun came clear, the corporal realized that Belle had not even attempted to draw her Dance. Instead she drew back her right leg, maintaining her balance with grace and agility. Straightening out her left leg, she raised herself on to her toes so as to gain added power to the right as it swung forward and up. Her toes caught the corporal's hand just as the Colt came out. Giving a yelp of surprise and pain, he lost his hold on the gun. His troubles did not end there.

In a continuation of the kick, Belle came down to both feet, rotated her body in a swift pivot and delivered a rear stamping kick to the man's stomach. Although she used less than her full strength, Belle doubled the startled soldier over. Again Belle pivoted, her right hand raising, clenched into a fist, and driving down so its heel struck the back of the man's neck and sent him to his knees. Stepping back, Belle drew and cocked her Dance.

"Well?" she asked.

Roars of laughter greeted her actions and the corporal looked up with a rueful grin. "Reckon this's no place for a *man*," he said. "You wouldn't've fooled Cap'n Dusty that way, I bet, ma'am."

"Not being fooled is why he's the captain and you're only a corporal," Billy Jack pointed out.

"How about it, Dusty?" asked Belle.

"You've made your point," Dusty answered with a grin. "You ride with my party. Now if you've finished fooling about, we'll go through the plan again."

## CHAPTER FOUR

## Captain Fog's Plan

Even though he approached the section of the Crossland Trace known as the Funnel, Captain Christie of the 6th New Jersey Dragoons felt neither concern nor apprehension for the safety of the visiting general entrusted to his care.

Some freak of nature had left a curious land formation at that point of the Trace. The gash carved into the land by innumerable wagon wheels and horses' hooves passed along the bottom of a valley towards a high, sheer cliff to wind through a narrow gorge which alone gave access to the land beyond the cliff. The valley itself had wooded slopes, but a good hundred yards of clear, open land separated the woods from the trail and, in Christie's considered opinion, rendered unlikely the chances of a successful ambush.

Riding slightly to the rear of the general's wagon, in a position which kept himself under the view of the senior officer while giving the appearance of being entirely occupied with the work of ensuring his charge's safety, Christie looked back at his command. A large company, sixty in strength, armed with Springfield carbines and Army Colts, strung out behind the general's carriage made an impressive and comforting sight. Only a good-sized confederate force would risk attacking so many men, Christie decided, and he doubted if a rebel outfit of any size could come so far north into Union-held territory. So he kept all his command riding in four smart, military-looking columns which ought to please the general, and ignored the suggestion his sergeant-major made about sending scouts ahead or putting flanking details out to search the wooded slopes.

Christie was one of a new breed of officer the War brought into the Union Army. Before the outbreak of hostilities, the South provided the majority of officers for the army, but most of them left to join their seceding states when the War began. Faced with a shortage of officers, the Union had to accept many men who would never have made the grade in the strict days before the War. Christie was one of them. Not that he originally intended to become a soldier. An interest in politics and a hatred for anyone who did not blindly conform to his beliefs made a patriot out of him. Having a prominent member of the Radical Republican Party for a father, Christie received acceptance and faster promotion than his talents merited. However, one needed to come into the eye of senior authority to rise higher than a captain, even in war-time. Coming into the eye could be done in two ways, by courage and endeavour on the battlefield, or by showing to good advantage in some general's presence. Not wishing to risk his valuable neck in action, Christie chose the latter. By waving his father's influence, he gained command of the escort for General Main, and to prevent anyone sharing the limelight, he left his second-in-command at the regiment's headquarters.

Day-dreaming of a rosy future when, on Main's recommendation, he reached field rank, Christie rode towards the

opening of the gorge. Suddenly his pleasant thoughts were
shattered by a series of wild, ringing yells and a scattering
of shots from the rear. Turning in his saddle, he saw something which sent a shock of apprehension through him.
Having a firm belief that he was destined to do great things
in the improvement of his country, Christie avoided taking
risks and had never been in action. For a moment his
numbed mind failed to function as he watched the grey-clad
riders burst from the left side of the trail some distance behind
the end of his column.

Fortunately for Christie, his sergeant-major was an old
soldier. Christie always regarded the non-com as a semi-
illiterate fool who came into the army because he could
not hold down any other work, but at that moment the
captain could have fallen on the other's neck in joy.

"Driver, move that carriage on the gallop!" the sergeant-major roared. "First three files follow it. Remainder
form line. Dismount. Prepare to fight on foot."

Although Christie had laid down instructions for action
in case of an attack, he could not collect his thoughts in
time to give them. Even the sergeant-major might have
failed had the rebels come in with a silent rush instead of
yelling and firing shots prematurely.

Typical of his type of mentality, Christie had been a
martinet who drove the men under him rather than leading
them. In this instance the driving bore fruit. Long hours of
drill had taught the men in the escort to react almost instinctively on hearing commands. The carriage's driver
swung his whip and urged his four-horse team forward at
an increasing pace into the mouth of the gorge, followed
by a sergeant and the first three files of four men from the
column. The remainder of the escort worked fast, swinging
their horses into line across the mouth of the gorge. On
dismounting, one man in six grabbed hold of the reins of
the other five's horses to leave the five free to fight. That
had become standard U.S. Army tactics, although Christie

trained his men in what he regarded as an improvement on normal procedure.

Most cavalry outfits had one man in four holding the horses. Christie decided that one in six would give him more men to fight and trained his company accordingly, putting the sergeant-major's tentative objections down to the stagnated thinking of a limited military mentality. Certainly the system showed its merit as the horse-holders grabbed their companions' reins and backed off to leave five, not three, men facing the enemy.

Standing in the centre of his men, Christie gave a superior smile as he watched the rebel cavalry mill uncertainly just beyond pistol range. To Christie that only went to prove his theories. It was so like the decadent Southerners to botch a good chance, then show cowardice in the face of a determined enemy. So thought Christie, nerve coming back as he saw the danger diminish. All he needed to do was keep his men in position and hold the rebels back until the carriage gained a good lead, then mount up and follow.

At Christie's side, the sergeant-major watched the rebels also, but felt very disturbed at what he saw. Unlike his officer, the non-com had seen action and knew a thing or two. So he wondered why such a troop as the one facing them would make a damned fool mistake like spoiling what would have been a first-class surprise attack by premature yelling and shooting. Although about half the size of the Yankee escort, that many men would still need to know their business to penetrate so far into Union territory undetected. Such skill did not mix with blundering incompetence or reluctance to fight, both of which the rebels had apparently shown.

Even as the sergeant-major opened his mouth to mention his fears to Christie, he heard the crack of a rifle shot from the right side of the slope almost level with his escort. A croaking gasp came from behind the sergeant-major and he twisted around to see one of the horse-holders collapse, bullet in head and hand opening to release the reins it held.

More shots crackled from the trees and the non-com estimated that at least five rifles covered them. A small force, until he realized what the riflemen's position and purpose meant. The shooting of the horse-holder had been no accident. Another two of the men holding the horses took lead, releasing their charges. More bullets screamed down, the loose horses began to mill and scatter, making their riders forget fighting and try to catch them.

Seeing the danger, the sergeant-major yelled orders for a party of men to make an attack on the attackers among the trees. As he started to move forward to give direction to the counter measures, a bullet caught him in the chest, spun him around and dropped him to the ground. Another horse-holder screamed an instant later, fell and allowed a further six animals to add to the confusion.

Up among the trees, Kiowa swung his rifle down after dropping the sergeant-major. The lean scout and his four-man detail—selected as being the best rifle-shots in the company and armed with Sharps, Henry or Spencer long guns "borrowed" from the Yankees—worked with deadly precision, following Dusty's orders.

On their arrival at the Funnel that morning, Dusty's men had been put into their positions and given a final run-through of their orders. On examining the area in which he would operate, Kiowa added a touch of his own to his leader's plans. After dropping the sergeant-major, Kiowa prepared to put his own touch into action.

Near where Kiowa knelt in the shelter and concealment of a slippery elm, a couple of springy young saplings had been bent over, their upper foliage stripped away and the tops secured by ropes. Balanced upon forks at the upper end of each sapling rested a Katchum four-pounder hand grenade, its percussion-cap fuse ready in place. Kiowa threw a glance at the saplings, rested his Henry against the elm and yelled:

"Now!"

Drawing his sheathed bowie knife, Kiowa sprang to the nearer sapling and one of his men leapt to the other. Razor-sharp steel sliced through the retaining ropes. While the spring of the saplings' rise to an upright position did not have the force to hurl the grenades the hundred yards or so which separated the rebels from the Trace, it flung the missile far farther than any human hand could. Downwards curved first one, then the other grenade. The firing mechanism, a tube of soft metal with a flange at its outer end and a percussion cap at the other, drove into the ground. A dull roar shattered the air, drowning any other sound for a moment, then a second explosion heralded the arrival of the other grenade.

Already spooked by the shooting and noise around them and disturbed by seeing others of their kind milling about, the horses still held by the remaining men assigned to that duty began to fight to escape. At that moment the sense of the Army's methods showed. One man could just about handle four horses during the heat of action; he had no chance of restraining six battle-scared animals, especially when under fire directed at him.

Struck by a careering horse, two men staggered and dropped their carbines. Other men forgot their duties as they tried to grab at passing animals. Complete chaos, of a kind only a real efficient leader could halt, reigned among the Dragoons, and Christie found his theories of how to handle men completely inadequate faced with the grim realities of war. The remaining horse-holders, realizing that their fellow workers had not been shot by accident, discarded their duty and turned free the struggling, terrified horses.

At which moment, following on the heels of the grenades' explosion, Red Blaze gave the order to his party to attack. Cutting through the wild, rebel yells, came the music of the bugle sounding the charge. Like puppets when the handler works the strings, every Texan's horse sprang forward in a disciplined rush at the disorganized Dragoons. And this time the Texans came on, determined to force home their charge. Reins looped around saddlehorns, leaving the riders' hands free to handle weapons, guiding their horses by knee-pressure, the Texans came down shooting and adding to the confusion already rampant among their enemies.

Even then a good commander might have rallied his men and saved the situation, for the Dragoons still outnumbered the Texans by almost two to one. Christie never even gave the matter a thought as panic gripped him. All his superiority over the common herd left him; his bombast about the damned cowardly rebel scum forgotten as he watched the wave of grey-clad riders pouring down towards him. Thrusting away his revolver, he sprang for and managed to catch the reins of a passing horse. Once in the saddle, he deserted his men and knocked down a corporal who was trying to rally a defence against the Texans' charge.

While Red Blaze might be a reckless young cuss with a penchant for becoming involved in any fight he might witness, he possessed one prime virtue which few people, himself included, knew about. Dusty knew it and was aware that given a responsible task Red became the coolest, steadiest hand a man could ask for. So even in the heady excitement of the charge, Red did not forget Dusty's orders.

"Stop that officer escaping, Bucky!" he yelled.

"Yo!" whooped a corporal at the end of the line and swung his horse away so that it charged up the slope at an angle which brought it towards the fleeing Christie.

Shock and terror came to Christie's face as he saw the Texan boiling up the slope towards him. Then the courage of a cornered rat sent Christie's hand to his holstered Colt. Twice the Texan's revolver spat, but the lead missed and Christie brought up his weapon. The courses of the two horses converged rapidly and Christie fired wildly, to make the fatal mistake of missing. Again the Texan squeezed his Army Colt's trigger, and at a range from which he stood little or no chance of missing. Searing agony ripped into Christie as he felt the shocking impact of striking lead. The gun fell from his hand and he slid from his horse to crash to the ground. On raced Christie's mount, heading up the slope at a gallop, but the Texan let it go. Having done his part in halting the officer's escape, the Texan swung his mount and rejoined his command.

A condition of wild confusion reigned among the Dragoons as they made an attempt to fight back against the on-rushing rebels. Men yelled, tried to use their guns, but were hampered by others of their party trying to capture mounts, or by the horses scattering through their ranks in wild stampede.

Demoralized by the loss of any guiding force—Red's men knew their business and cut down any Yankee who showed signs of organizing a defence against them—the Dragoons needed only the sight of Christie deserting them to save his own neck to make them decide that they had had enough of war. Unfortunately escaping did not prove easy for the Yankees as Kiowa's party had performed their assigned duty very well. So well that not a single horse-holder still retained a grip of any of his comrades' mounts, although a few did keep a grip of their own animals. Not that the possession would do any good for them. Following Dusty's orders and Red's reminders, the Texans cut down any man who tried to escape.

"Don't shoot!" yelled one of the Dragoons, throwing aside his unfired Springfield carbine. "I quit!"

Such action in a command as badly shaken as Christie's company was certain to prove infectious. Guns rained to the ground and arms shot into the air in surrender. A few of the harder souls, long-term soldiers who saw battle in Indian campaigns, might have fought it out, but most of them had already taken lead and the remainder recognized the futility of continuing the uneven struggle.

"Hold your fire!" Red's voice boomed out like a clarion call.

Bringing his men to a halt, Red wasted no time in self-congratulation at a very well handled piece of work. Yet he might have taken pride in his achievement, for he brought about the capture of an enemy force almost twice as large as his command, inflicting heavy casualties on the Yankees, without the loss or wounding of a single Texan. True the plan had been out of Dusty's fertile brain, but carrying it to its successful conclusion fell upon Red.

With the wild, heady excitement of the charge still throbbing through him, Red still retained enough command of himself to know what must be done. While the Yankees had shown every sign of surrender, giving them time to regain their senses or recover from their shock might have disastrous results. Even now Red's command was outnumbered by the enemy and up close could be badly mauled if some leader managed to rally the dispirited Yankees.

"Line them up, disarm them!" Red ordered.

Moving swiftly, yet with skilled precision that told of long practice, the Texans formed up the Dragoons in small parties and separated them from their weapons. Although the Springfield carbines were smashed beyond repair by beating against the ground, the Army Colts suffered no damage. To a rebel no piece of enemy property had so much attraction as those latest products from the Hartford factory of Colonel Samuel Colt and, while unwilling to weigh their mounts down with single-shot Springfield carbines, the Texans willingly added the burden of the Dragoon's revolvers.

While the disarming took place, Red recalled another section of the company.

"Kiowa!" he yelled.

"Yo!" came back the answer from the trees.

"You can come out now, we've done got them all hawg-tied down."

"That Red sure is a fighting son," grinned one of Kiowa's party as they went to collect their horses.

"He sure is," agreed another and threw a look at the captured Dragoons. "Man oh man, Cap'n Dusty's plan worked out real well."

"Now me," put in Kiowa dryly. "I'd've been more surprised if it *hadn't*."

# CHAPTER FIVE

## Captain Fog Acquires Wealth

From the front, the small knot of bushes looked natural enough, although the only growth of its kind anywhere nearer than a hundred yards from the trail at the western mouth of the Funnel. In fact until less than an hour before even that clump of bushes did not grow so close to the trail, having been cut higher up the left slope of the valley and replaced in the position Dusty Fog selected as best for his purpose. Lying behind the bushes, hidden from sight of anyone on the trail, Dusty watched the mouth of the Funnel for the first sight of the paymaster's carriage. Already he could hear shots in the distance and knew the first part of his plan had begun. Everything now depended on how well Belle Boyd had been able to learn about the character of the man commanding the paymaster's escort; and also on whether Dusty called the play right about how the Yankee commander would react to Red's attack.

Would the Yankee play into Dusty's hands by making a fight on foot across the eastern mouth of the Funnel, allowing the paymaster's carriage to build up a good start on any pursuit by the Texans? If the Yankee halted, might he not keep the carriage close at hand? If he sent it, how many men were likely to be in its escort?

On the answer to those questions hinged the success or failure of Dusty's strategy. Probably even more so than it rested upon his ability to hit a one-inch round mark at fifty yards with a borrowed Spencer carbine. Should the first part of his plans fail for any reason, Dusty would have no need to demonstrate his skill with a shoulder arm by hitting the detonator flange of the six-pounder Ketchum grenade facing him on the far side of the trail.

Every instinct Dusty possessed told him that the Yankee commander would act in the required manner. Even the crack U.S. Army outfits like Custer's 7th Michigan Cavalry only rarely fought in the saddle. By virtue of their training and traditions, the Dragoons always fought dismounted. Once the Yankees left their horses, Dusty knew he could rely on Red and Kiowa to handle their parts of the plan. Which left only Dusty and Belle to perform their assigned tasks for the affair to be brought to a successful conclusion.

For a moment Dusty wondered if he had done the correct thing in allowing Belle to take such an active part in what would be a dangerous business. Then he grinned as he decided that he had been given little or no choice in the matter. Taken all in all, that beautiful girl spy had a mighty persuasive way about her. More than that, his men admired her and regarded her as being lucky for them. During the long ride north to the Crossland Trace they had seen no sign of Yankees, even though the route they took led them within two miles of the Dragoons' camp at Russelville. Even the crossing of the Coon Fork of the Arkansas gave them no trouble due to Kiowa finding a shallows with a firm gravel bottom that offered good footing for the horses. Belle had proved herself capable and as good as any of the men at handling her horse, a thing which raised her even higher in the estimation of the Texans. So Dusty found that the men in the party he told Belle to join not only accepted her presence but appeared to let her take command in the place of a non-com.

Including Belle in one party had been caused by necessity. Three men guarded the two Yankee prisoners and the company's reserve horses some distance away in a valley bottom. Taking them away from the company as well as Kiowa's detail and the ten men Dusty required did not leave Red with many guns for his part of the plan. However, it had been amusing to see those five leathery soldiers, bone-tough fighting men all, show pleasure at having Belle with them and accepting her as their leader—or did they? One of the prime qualities of any fighting man was the ability to recognize a leader; and the Texans saw those qualities in Belle just as they recognized leadership in Dusty or Red.

Anyway, Dusty mused, it was long gone too late for him to think of changing his force around and sending the girl to the safety of the prisoner-guarding detail.

As if giving definite proof that it was indeed too late for a change, Dusty heard the growing rumble of hooves and steel-rimmed wheels upon confined hard rock. He still could not see the paymaster's carriage, nor, due to the deflection and distortion caused by the Funnel's walls, form any kind of guess how many horses approached. Not that Dusty wasted time in idle conjecture.

On hearing the sound, Dusty eased forward the Spencer carbine and rested its barrel upon the crown of his hat which lay ready for that purpose upon a rock before him. So carefully had he selected his position and arranged the cover that, although he could take a good aim at the trail, no part of himself or the carbine showed beyond the bushes. Closing his left eye, Dusty took careful aim at the triangle of light-coloured rocks which showed plainly at the far side of the trail. Slowly he moved down the tip of the foresight so that centred on the black circle of the Ketchum's detonator flange in the middle of the triangle. While the Spencer could not be classed with the latest model Sharps rifle in the accuracy line, Dusty figured that its twenty-inch barrel ought to send a four-hundred-grain .56 calibre bullet right where aimed at fifty yards, even if the propellant power be only fifty grains of powder.

A quick glance showed Dusty that the carriage had burst into sight at the mouth of the Funnel. On its box the driver swung his whip and yelled encouraging curses at the four-horse team while a second soldier, riding as guard, lent a hand by pitching rocks at the team and added his quota of verbal inducement. Close behind the rocking, lurching coach came the escort: a sergeant and twelve men. Big odds against Dusty's party happen he failed to make good his shot at the Ketchum's detonator flange.

From the way it continued to race along, the carriage and escort did not intend to halt and await word of how the main body fared. That figured, knowing the consignment the Yankee general carried in the carriage. He would want to build up as good a lead as possible in case the Texans broke through the rearguard defence of the main body. Well, maybe he would not want to desert his companions, but clearly intended to do his duty by keeping moving.

Dusty settled down, cuddling the stock of the Spencer against his shoulder and laying the carbine, setting the tip of the foresight's blade exactly in the centre of the back sight's V notch and aligning them carefully on the black dot at which he aimed. For a moment the team horses and carriage hid his mark from sight and the dust churned up by hooves and wheels masked it. Holding his fire, Dusty did not panic even though he knew what depended on his making a hit. The escort did not ride right up to the carriage, but stayed far enough back to keep an uninterrupted view of the trail and valley ahead. Brief though the gap might be, it gave Dusty just enough time. The dust cleared and he saw his mark, finding as he hoped that his aim still held on it. Without fluster he squeezed the trigger. The

Spencer barked, belched flame and sent its bullet hurtling out.

An instant later, with a dull roar and burst of flame, scattering fragments of metal casing and surrounding rocks in a deadly fountain, the Ketchum exploded. Dusty's bullet must have almost touched the sergeant's horse in passing, for the animal caught the full force of the explosion, both it and its rider going down in a hideously torn mass of lacerated flesh and spurting blood. The blast swept the nearer two men of the leading file from their horses, tumbled the third out of his saddle and threw the remainder of the escort into confusion. Reining in desperately, trying to regain control of their plunging, terrified horses, the second file ploughed into the first, horses going down. One of the final file crashed into the jumble, a second pitched over his horse's head as it came to a sudden halt.

"Yeeah!"

Acting on their orders, five of Dusty's men burst into sight on the right side of the valley, making all the noise they could manage. Guns in hand, they tore down the slope towards the disorganized escort.

Only two of the escort avoided the tangled jumble, and they more through luck than by good management. Wild with terror inspired by the explosions, screams and stench of spilled blood, the horses reared, fought and finally bolted to the left, headed in Dusty's direction.

On firing his shot, Dusty started to work the Spencer's loading lever and at the same moment thrust himself rapidly out of his cover. He knew that none of the Dragoons must be allowed to escape, but could not handle the Spencer freely enough from his hiding place to rely on taking his share in bottling in the Yankees. Both the approaching Dragoons appeared to be good horsemen and were already gaining control of their mounts. Seeing Dusty, and guessing that it was he who detonated the explosion, they charged in his direction. One of the pair drew his Army Colt and fired at Dusty, but thirty yards was too great a range for a man to perform accurate shooting with a handgun when astride a racing horse. Drawing back the Spencer's side-hammer, Dusty threw the carbine to his shoulder, took aim and touched off a shot in return. Caught in the shoulder by the heavy bullet, the eager Dragoon pitched out of the saddle, his gun dropping from his hand.

Ignoring his fallen comrade, the second man continued his charge and drew his gun. From all appearances he was an old soldier and well-versed in his business. Not for him to open fire wildly at a range where luck alone might guide home the bullet. Instead he headed straight for Dusty, meaning to ride the other down and end the affair at a distance from which he could hardly miss.

Dusty worked the lever of the Spencer, feeling the breach start to open, stick for an instant, then came back —only no empty cartridge case flicked into the air. Metal cartridge manufacture had not yet developed to a stage where reliable cases were the rule rather than the exception and accidents frequently happened. Even without looking, Dusty guessed that the case had stuck tighter than usual in the chamber and the withdrawing ejector tore its head off, leaving the remainder of the brass cyclinder inside the gun and effectively preventing the insertion of a replacement bullet.

Nearer rushed the Dragoon, still holding his fire. Dusty's right hand left the Spencer, driving down and across his body in a move almost too fast for the eye to follow. Trained fingers curled around the waiting white handle of the left-side Colt and its streamlined length flowed from the holster. Back drew the hammer under Dusty's thumb and his forefinger slipped into the trigger-guard. He did not offer to raise the gun shoulder high and take sight in the formal manner; with the Dragoon rushing closer by the second there would not have been time. Not that Dusty needed to use a fancy duelling stance. He had been trained to handle his Colts in the manner of the Texas range country and down there if a man needed a gun, he mostly did not have time to adopt a fancy stance before using his weapon. Even as the Dragoon fired his opening shot, Dusty's Colt roared from waist high and aimed by instinctive alignment. Like Dusty figured, the Dragoon knew how to handle a gun. Only the fact that the man fired from a mighty unsteady platform saved Dusty; and at that the Dragoon's bullet stirred the Texan's hair in passing.

For his part, Dusty shot back the only way he dared under the circumstances—for a kill. There was no time for taking a careful aim and sending a bullet into the man's shoulder, not when faced with an enemy so skilled in use of a gun. So Dusty sent his bullet into the Dragoon's chest as offering the easiest target under the prevailing conditions. Jerking under the impact of the lead, the Dragoon let his gun drop and slid off his horse. So close had it been that Dusty was forced to throw himself aside to avoid being run down by the horse.

Down on the trail, the Dragoons had been too dazed and shocked to offer any resistance and, even as Dusty shot down the second man, were surrendering to his five Texans. One of the five, Dusty's company guidon carrier, wheeled away from the rest. Leading Dusty's stallion, as was his duty at such times, the guidon carrier loped over to where his captain waited. Dusty took the black's reins, mounted and turned his attention to where Belle's party intercepted the fleeing carriage.

"Steady!" Belle breathed as she watched the carriage hurl by the point where the Ketchum grenade awaited Dusty's bullet.

Around her, concealed among a clump of bushes, the five men assigned to take the carriage held their restive mounts in check. At Belle's side, the burly corporal whose challenge had brought a lesson in *savate*, gave the girl a grin. He volunteered to ride in her party with the express intention of showing Belle how it was done. Yet he, like the others, willingly accepted her as the leader.

All heard the crack of Dusty's Spencer followed by the roars as the Ketchum exploded.

"Charge!" Belle ordered, her voice low but urgent.

Setting her spurs to the flanks of her mount, she sent it leaping out of cover and down the slope. Dance in hand, she led the men towards the wagon in a fast and deadly rush. Yet they went in silence, without as much as a cowhand yell to give warning of their presence. Lack of cover caused Dusty to station the party farther from the trail than he wanted, but he tried to ease their task as much as possible.

Racing their horses downwards, Belle and the Texans watched the carriage for the first sign that its occupants noticed them. Seventy-five yards, fifty, thirty; still the driver and guard, watching the ambush of the remainder of their escort, failed to see or hear their danger. The hooves of their team and the rumbling of the wheels on the trail drowned out the grass-muffled drumming of the Texans' mounts. Even General Main stared back at the havoc Dusty's grenade caused among the Dragoons during the first, dangerous moments of the charge.

Suddenly the driver became aware that his team careered along the Trace without guidance from him. Twisting around, he prepared to handle the reins and saw the charging group. His warning yell, garbled though it came out, served to bring the guard's attention to the front. The warning came just too early for Belle's party to make a safe contact with the enemy.

Belle had chosen to wear her Union Army fatigue cap and taken with her dark blue shirt and black breeches it gave her the appearance of a Yankee soldier. Under the stress and excitement of the moment, the guard completely overlooked certain aspects of Belle's appearance which ought to have told him that he did not look at a man. To his eyes a member of his own army rode with the rebels; a traitor; a lousy, stinking renegade who had sold out to the enemy and brought death or injury to a good few Union soldiers that day. Fury boiled inside the guard and he swore to himself that he would get the damned traitor or want to know why not.

Although she saw the guard's eyes riveted on her, Belle felt no great anxiety at first. The Springfield carbine issued to the Union Army's enlisted man had never been a weapon noted for accuracy and she reckoned she could take a chance on the guard shooting at her from the swaying box of the racing carriage.

Only the guard did not hold an inaccurate Springfield carbine.

Apprehension ripped through Belle as she realized that the guard's weapon had two barrels. No matter how the box rocked, a ten-gauge shot-gun at that range would be unlikely to miss if its handler knew his business. From the smooth way the guard started to raise his shot-gun, Belle figured he knew enough to make things all-fired dangerous for anybody he aimed to hit.

At Belle's side, the burly corporal saw the raising of the shot-gun and with something of a shock realized that the guard aimed to cut the girl down. Swinging his horse, the corporal rammed it into Belle's racing bay and staggered the other animal aside. Flame tore from the shot-gun's right barrel as nine buckshot balls lashed from its muzzle in a spreading pattern of death. At twenty-five yards the balls had spread enough so that a human body would catch most of them—and the corporal had ridden into the place he knocked Belle from. Seven of the .32 calibre balls tore into his body. He jerked backwards, striking the cantle of his saddle. The army Colt slid from his fingers and he fell sideways to the ground. His four male companions fired back at the guard, but missed.

Only Belle's superb riding skill kept her in the saddle as her horse reeled under the impact of the corporal's charge. Not only did she retain her seat, but collected and brought the bay under control. At the same moment her brain

screamed a warning that she must do something or take the
shot-gun's left barrel's charge. The guard saw his first shot
miss the girl and wavered between which of the attackers
he ought to try next.

Much as she hated what she must do, that pause gave
Belle her chance. Bringing up the Dance, she threw a shot
at the nearest of the carriage's team. Even from the back
of the racing bay, Belle could hardly miss so large a target.
Screaming as the .36 ball hit it, the horse stumbled and
went down, bringing the other leader with it. Instantly the
carriage lurched to a violent halt. The guard's shot-gun
boomed, but as an involuntary measure as his finger tightened on the trigger when he was thrown forward. He hit
nothing and before he recovered took a bullet from one of
the Texans.

The driver could do nothing beyond trying to keep himself from being thrown off the box and also prevent his
team from killing each other or themselves in their wild
panic. Inside the coach General Main had been pitched
forward, his head smashing into the side. Blackness welled
over him and he collapsed to the floor.

Leaving the men to handle the carriage's driver and oc-
cupant, Belle whirled her bay around in a rump-scraping
turn and left the saddle before the animal stopped. She
holstered her Dance as she ran to where the corporal lay
sprawled on the ground. Dropping to her knees beside the
stricken man, she gently raised his head and pillowed it
upon her knees. For a moment she thought he was dead,
then his eyes opened and he looked at her. A pain-wracked
grin twisted his lips.

"Reckon I put one over on—you—this—time—
ma'am!" he gasped.

Before Belle could make any reply, she saw his body
stiffen, blood oozed out of his mouth and his eyes glazed
over, then the body went limp. For the first time in three or
more years Belle felt the impact of death. She knew that
she owed the corporal her life. If he had not knocked her

horse aside, it would be she who lay on the ground. Tears trickled down Belle's cheeks and she remained on her knees, cradling the soldier's dead head in her hands.

Hooves drummed behind Belle but she did not look up to see who approached.

"How is he?" asked Dusty's voice.

Turning, Belle looked up at the small Texan. Grief showed plainly on her face and she replied, "He's dead. Died saving me."

"Poor old Mike," Dusty said, his voice gentle. "He was a good soldier."

The corporal had also been a good friend in the days before the War, companion on more than one schoolboy escapade. However, Dusty had long since learned that friends died in battle, but that life must go on. The lives of the rest of the company depended on Dusty, so he must hold down his sorrow at losing a friend and force himself to go ahead with the work at hand.

"I'll send somebody to tend to him," Dusty told Belle. "Come and help me find the money."

Gently Belle laid the still form on the ground and came to her feet. Looking around, she found everything under control. Already Dusty's party had joined the men who rode with her. The Yankee prisoners stood to one side under guard and attended to their wounded. On Dusty's orders, two of the Texans came forward to load the dead corporal on his horse. Back at the reserve horses, one of the packs, carried a couple of shovels with which a grave could be dug. At the carriage, the driver, now disarmed, and a Texan helped a dazed, bloody-scalped, groaning General Main from inside.

"Have you pulled the General's teeth?" asked Dusty.

"Sure have, Cap'n," grinned the Texan and held up one of the small, metal-cartridge Smith and Wesson revolvers which had become popular with members of the U.S. Army assigned to more sedentary duties. "Ain't this the fiercest gun you ever did see though."

The hoots of derisive laughter which rose from the other Texans, firm .44 calibre addicts who regarded even the .36 Navy bullets as being a mite small for *serious* work, did nothing to make them relax their vigilance or control of their prisoners. Although Dusty held the same views as his men, he stopped their comments with a low growled word.

"Rider coming fast, Cap'n Dusty," announced one of the men.

"It's Kiowa," another went on.

Bringing his horse to a halt by the carriage, Kiowa threw a quick glance around, nodded with satisfaction, then reported to Dusty.

"Went off right as right could be. Red's marching the Yankees through the Funnel right now."

"Any casualties—" asked Dusty.

"None. Leastways, not on our side."

"Good," Dusty said and turned to look in the direction of the Funnel. Then he swung back and watched two of his men, under Belle's urgings, removing a large box from the carriage.

"This's what I wanted, Dusty," the girl breathed.

Something in her attitude drew Dusty's eyes to Belle. Mere lust for money did not give her the air of excitement. True she would probably receive a percentage of the consignment as a reward for her efforts, but he knew patriotism and not profit had been her motive.

Drawing his right-hand Colt, he sent a bullet into the lock, shattering it. Belle threw back the lid and looked at the canvas bags. Taking one out, she borrowed Kiowa's knife and slit it open. Gold coins glinted in her hands and she raised her eyes to Dusty's.

"How do we transport the money?" she asked. "The carriage won't help us."

"Never aimed to use it," Dusty replied. We'll make up the money into loads for two pack-horses. Then I'll send

Kiowa and Red to escort you back to our headquarters. Reckon Uncle Devil'll see that you get where you want to go after that."

"Can't you come with me?"

"Reckon not. I don't know how soon the Yankees will learn about this raid, but I do know it'll make them potboiling wild when they hear. So I figured to keep my boys in this area, stir things up just like I was sent to do."

"That'll be risky," Belle pointed out.

"Sure," Dusty agreed. "But maybe they'll figure I've still got the money with me and give you an easy trip through. Anyways, I've got to try to draw as much of the Yankee strength as possible up here so that Cousin Buck has a better chance of taking that supply depot and getting Company A out alive."

Much as Belle wanted to ask Dusty to come back with her, she did not. She knew the dangers of her own task and needed help, but a whole company of the Texas Light Cavalry might be wiped out if Dusty failed to do his part in a large plan. Making a swift calculation, Belle decided that she had a few days to spare even allowing for travelling time.

"How long will you be out?" she asked.

"Two days, should be back at headquarters in four," Dusty replied, wondering at her questions.

"I may see you there then," Belle smiled.

"Likely," agreed Dusty and turned back to attend to preparations for joining Red and pulling out.

## CHAPTER SIX

## A Furlough For Captain Fog

"Lawsy me, Cap'n Dusty, sah," greeted the fat, jovial-looking Negro butler as he opened the front doors of the big house taken over by the Texas Light Cavalry for their officers' mess. "You-all looks all peaked, gaunt and tired."

"I feel a mite that way, Oscar," Dusty replied.

Since parting from Red, Belle and Kiowa, Dusty had been constantly on the move. By pushing his men and horses to the very limits of their endurance, he stirred up a hornet's nest in the north-west Arkansas and left the Yankees feeling that they had been hit by a raging Texas-twister in all its fury. An unexpected evening rush took the reinforced guard at the Coon Fork bridge by surprise, coming as it did from the northern bank of the river. After destroying the Vandenburg gun—the horses were too tired and in no shape to haul such a valuable piece of booty back to the Confederate lines—Dusty's men crossed the bridge and destroyed it behind them. The rest had been fairly easy. Walking more than they rode their leg-weary horses, the men made for and crossed the Ouachita, then passed through Confederate-held territory to their regiment's headquarters.

Already the men had attended to their horses and saddles, cleaned their weapons, ate a good meal and now prepared to catch up on some badly needed sleep. Dusty knew that before he could think of resting he still had to make his reports, write at least one of the letters to the parents of the seven men who died on the mission, and clean his Colts. No man who lived as Dusty did ever failed to take *that* precaution.

"I'll want some boiling water sent up to my room after I've seen Colonel Blaze, Oscar," he told the butler.

"If it am boiling, it ain't for washing," the Negro answered. "And if it's for cleaning your guns, I'd sure admire for you-all to do it outside. It sure makes the room smell something wild if you-all does it indoors."

"Reckon you're right at that," Dusty smiled. "Have it out back of the kitchen in fifteen minutes."

Big, burly, yet hard-fleshed and capable-looking, Colonel Blaze saw Dusty immediately. One glance told Blaze that his nephew had been hard-travelled and looked in need of sleep.

"Make it short, boy," Blaze ordered. "I'll have the full story later."

Taking the chair brought up by the sergeant who showed him into the room, Dusty sank down with a low sigh of contentment. Then he shook off the lethargy and said, "You'll know about the gold consignment, sir?"

"Red brought it in two days ago. They had to lay up north of the Ouachita for a day because of Yankee activity stopping them crossing."

"Pleased they made it. Where's Red now?"

"I sent him out on a foraging expedition, we need meat and the next shipment of beef hasn't come in from home yet," Blaze grinned. "Had to give him something to do or he'd've been heading back across the Ouachita to look for you. Damned short on discipline that boy. Takes after his pappy."

Dusty grinned and let the statement ride, knowing that the Colonel had high regard for Red's sterling qualities and meant nothing by his growled-out tirade. Wanting to get through so that he could finish his other work, and catch some sleep, Dusty told his uncle of his company's activities after separating from Red. At last Blaze nodded with satisfaction. From what Dusty told him, the stirring-up process had worked real well.

"I expect Major Amesley'll want your report in writing, Dustine," he said. "But see to it after you've had some sleep."

"Yo!" Dusty replied, rising and saluting.

On leaving the colonel's office, Dusty went through the rear of the building and found, as he expected, a bowl of boiling water waiting for him. Already his striker had taken his saddle to his room and brought down the box with cleaning gear for the guns.

Normally Dusty would not have thought of emptying both his guns at the same time, but he figured that in the safety of his regimental headquarters he could dispense with the precaution of always keeping one weapon ready for use. Unbuckling his gunbelt, he removed and laid it on the small table by the wall. After taking off his hat and jacket, he put them with the belt. He drew the two revolvers from their holsters and carried them to the table in the centre of the yard, putting one down by the steaming bowl of water while he prepared to clean the other.

While the 1860 Army Colt could truthfully claim to be the finest fighting handgun of its day, hard-hitting, accurate, robots and well-constructed, if only functioned correctly when given proper care and attention. Since the correct functioning of his guns could mean the difference between life and death, Dusty always devoted time to their maintenance. After a prolonged period of regular use, like the past few days had called for, more than a mere cleansing of the barrel and cylinder's chambers was necessary.

After setting the right-hand Colt at half cock, Dusty took the basic precaution of removing the percussion caps from the cylinder nipples. Not until he had guarded against accidental discharge did he drive out the wedge which held the barrel and cylinder on the lock frame's base pin. Turning the cylinder slightly, he worked the ramming lever under the barrel so that its head pressed against the partition between two of the chambers and so forced the barrel free from the base pin. Next he removed the cylinder from the base pin and carefully worked the bullets out of the chambers. Although the base of each paper cartridge had been torn on loading, to facilitate the ignition of the enclosed charge, the powder could be used again and the lead remoulded into fresh bullets; so Dusty made sure he drew each load correctly and set them where they would be safe from splashing water. Placing the barrel and empty cylinder into the water, he turned his attention to the lock frame.

Pieces of exploding percussion caps often worked down into the mechanism of the gun, and a careful man removed them regularly. It said much for the ingenuity of the Army Colt's designer that the mechanism was so simple an ordinary user could strip and assemble it without needing to call upon the service of a trained gunsmith. Using the screwdriver which came in the case with his guns, Dusty removed the three screws holding the butt grips in place. He then unfastened the screw which connected the main spring to the triggerguard and turned the spring from under the hammer's tumbler. Removing three more screws allowed him to take off the triggerguard and he twisted away another to gain access to the double spring which bore on the trigger and bolt. Next he removed the trigger and bolt by unfastening two screw-pins. Lastly he released the screw-pin which allowed him to withdraw the hammer, its hand still attached, downwards through the lock frame.

With that done, Dusty set to work on the second Colt, repeating the process and finally started to give every part a thorough cleaning. While working, he heard footsteps approaching and looked up at a man and a girl who came towards him. For a moment he hardly recognized Belle Boyd, as she wore a stylish grey dress and a large-brimmed hat from under which hung long red hair. At her side strode General Ole Devil Hardin. Tall, ramrod straight, immaculate in his uniform of a full general of the Confederate States Army, Hardin's lean, tanned face had the look of a hard disciplinarian tempered with a sense of humour. His face showed no expression, but relief glinted in his usually hard black eyes as he studied his illustrious nephew.

"Carry on with your work, Dustine," Hardin greeted as Dusty lowered the lock-frame in preparation to render military courtesy by coming to attention and saluting. "Pleased to see you back, boy."

"So am I, Dusty," Belle went on, trying to sound formal but belying the effort with her warm smile.

"Which same makes three of us," Dusty answered with a faint grin.

"Rough trip, boy?" asked Ole Devil.

The grin died away and Dusty nodded his head. "Rough enough, sir, I lost seven men when we tangled with a battalion of Yankee cavalry. Had to run near on four miles before we lost him. I think they were the 8th Pennsylvania Regiment."

Which, as Hardin knew, meant that the Yankees did belong to the regiment named. Dusty was well enough schooled in his work to know the need for accurate identification of an enemy force.

"Good," Hardin growled. "The 8th are based to the east. You've pulled out at least some of them and will have everybody's attention on the west."

"I hope so, sir," Dusty replied. "Cousin Buck will have it hard enough on his assignment. Anything I could do will help him a mite." He paused for a moment, giving his attention to cleaning the lock-frame, then went on, "What's next for me, sir?"

"How's your company?"

"Horses are about done, but a few days will see them right, or we can draw from the regiment's remounts."

"It's time your men came off active duties for a time," Old Devil stated, having already seen the condition of the horses Dusty brought back from the patrol. "How'd you like a furlough, boy?"

"Back home in Texas, sir?" asked Dusty, trying hard to hide the eagerness in his voice.

" 'Fraid not. In Matamoros."

Using a rod, Dusty fished one of the barrels from the water. His eyes went first to the girl, then swung back to Ole Devil. "Matamoros in Mexico, sir?"

"If there's another, we're not interested in it," Ole Devil replied, watching Dusty start to clean the barrel. "It's a right lively place for a young feller to spend a furlough in, or so they tell me."

"And if it's any inducement, Dusty," Belle put in. "I'll be going there with you."

"Why not tell me the *assignment,* sir," Dusty suggested.

Turning his grim face towards Belle, Ole Devil smiled one of his rare smiles, "I told you we might as well lay our cards straight on the table, Miss Boyd."

"It's usually the best," she agreed. "Only in my line one gets used to taking the long way around." She turned back to Dusty and watched him thrusting the cleaning rod through the Colt's barrel while its head dried the moisture from it, "You see, Dusty, I'm taking that Yankee gold to Matamoros and I'd naturally prefer to have a reliable escort along with me."

"The town's lively all right, Dustine," Old Devil continued. "A lot of our people went down there when the Yankees took over Brownsville. Then deserters from both sides began to trickle in. All the usual type of riff-raff and adventurers have moved there, it serves as a handy point for smuggling blockade-run goods into Texas and that game doesn't attract many saints. Then there's the French garrison and most likely a fair amount of Mexicans who are getting ready for the big rebellion that's brewing down there against Maximilian . . ."

"You're forgetting somebody, General," Belle stated.

"Who, ma'am?"

"Yankee spies. Pinkerton runs a mighty efficient organization and won't have overlooked a good bet like Matamoros."

"He'll likely have them there," Dusty agreed, "and in touch with the U.S. Navy ships on blockade service along the Texas coast. All in all, I can think of a whole heap safer places to take the gold."

"That's why Miss Boyd wants an escort, Dustine," Ole Devil said.

"Preferably you, Dusty," Belle went on.

"I'm game, if that's the way you want it, sir," Dusty answered.

"Damn it, that's *not* the way I want it. But with a shipment of arms due to arrive at Matamoros in the near future, I'd like to see the South lay its hands on them."

"So that's it," Dusty breathed, then raised the barrel and looked through its now shining bore.

"The shipment is one I arranged for in England just before I left," Belle explained. "The man gathering it is not one of our supporters, but a merchant captain with a shady reputation. Normally when he insisted on payment in gold, I would have ignored the offer, especially with the conditions he laid down. But I saw the consignment. New Enfield rifles—"

"Which are as good guns as a man could ask for," Dusty interrupted. "For infantrymen that is."

"Better than anything we have from our own sources," Belle replied. "He is also supplying a large quantity of ammunition and British powder is the best in the world. The consignment is worth the money."

"You saw the consignment?" asked Dusty.

"And had it checked by a gunsmith."

"Why is there such a delay in his arriving at Mata-moros, and why go there instead of running the blockade to bring the guns into a Southern port?"

On hearing Dusty's questions, Belle felt certain she had done the right thing in requesting that the small Texan be appointed her escort for what she knew must be a danger-ous mission. Clearly he aimed to take nothing, not even her loyalty, to chance; and she admired him for his caution.

"Captain Smee, the owner of the consignment, is no supporter of the Confederate States, which is why he says he will deliver to Matamoros rather than risk running the blockade. As for the delay, his ship is in dry-dock receiv-ing a thorough re-fit after damage gained, I feel sure, in some illegal enterprise. He is quite willing to sell his arms to us, but only if we come to Matamoros for them. In Matamoros he can find other customers. The Mexicans fighting to establish one of their own in command as *Pre-sidente* could use those arms. So could the French army of occupation. Even the Yankees would buy the consignment rather than see it fall into our hands."

"I think of four, that jasper Smee would rather sell to us," Ole Devil commented. "The Mexicans might like the arms, but I doubt if they've the kind of money to pay for it. As the French can have arms shipped from France at less cost, they won't go so high. Maybe the Yankees would buy the shipment. In fact they're certain to try. They can use those arms just as well as we could. So I want that ship-ment in our hands, Dustine."

"That figures, sir," Dusty said quietly, for he knew the situation well.

"Smee has done this sort of thing before, though not dealing with us," Belle continued. "The arms are packed in boxes marked "Farm Machinery" or something equally in-nocent. Not that he needs to go to any great lengths."

"The Yankees control Brownsville and can cover the mouth of the Rio Grande," Dusty warned. "And they've blockade-ships in the area."

"But Smee sails under the British flag," Belle pointed out.

At that time Britain was still *the* major world power and sane heads in the Federal Government fought shy of antagonizing the great country across the Atlantic. Opinion in Britain still remained sharply divided on whether to give active support to North or South in the War. A chance insult, an affront against the Union Jack, would give added weight to the arguments of the interests favouring the South. Earlier in the War, a Yankee naval ship's interference with British merchantmen on the high seas caused a diplomatic storm that only considerable tact and some concessions prevented from developing into anything worse. So while under the laws of war ships of a blockading squadron had the right to search neutral vessels trying to enter an enemy port, Matamoros lay in the territory of a neutral nation and the Yankees had no right to interfere with a British ship making for it.

"Which means the Yankees will either have to stop us buying the consignment," said Ole Devil, "or prevent us from receiving it after the purchase. Miss Boyd will handle the purchase, Dustine. But it will fall on you to ensure its safe delivery. I won't tell you how to accomplish that. It will depend on conditions in Matamoros."

"It won't be easy, sir," Dusty replied.

"I know. That's why I'm allowing you to take Mr. Blaze with you."

"Red?"

"He was christened Charles William Henry," Ole Devil growled dryly.

"Reckon *he* remembers that, sir?" grinned Dusty. "Who'll be commanding the Company while we're away?"

Due to their considerable successes in the field and the fact that they handled most of the difficult raiding chores for the regiment, Company C regarded themselves as the élite of the élite; a crack fighting outfit pride of achievement to boost them. Such men regarded their officers as being only one shade lower than God and would never take to following any other leaders without considerable fuss. Any officer placed in command of Company C, even temporarily, would have a restive outfit to control until he won their respect. Another point Ole Devil had to remember was that all the men capable of taking over Company C, and making a go of it, already ran their own companies and would not care to change. However, the General knew the only way out of his difficulty.

"I'm putting your father in command," he replied.

Dusty's father, Hondo Fog, held rank of major and acted as second-in-command of the Texas Light Cavalry. With his forceful personality he could take over Dusty's company and maintain it as the small Texan would wish.

"It's time Company C came off active duty anyway," Ole Devil went on. "I'll keep them around the camp. A spell of guard detail, drill and work here won't hurt them."

It would also give the outfit time to catch up on their rest and allow the horses to regain that peak of condition so necessary in the work Company C handled. Dusty felt relieved to know that his men would not be on patrol while he went on the assignment to Matamoros.

"How do we get there, sir?" he asked.

At that moment Hardin saw the fatigue-lines on Dusty's face. "Damn it, boy!" he barked. "Leave it until tomorrow. Finish cleaning your guns and then go get some sleep. That's an order."

Dusty nodded in agreement. That was one order he intended to carry out.

## CHAPTER SEVEN

## Disturbing News For Miss Boyd

*"And in conclusion, I say again how deeply grieved I am at having to send you this news, and how I sympathize with you in your loss; but I repeat that your son died gallantly while performing his duty and in so doing helped to save the lives of his comrades.*

> *Yours sincerely,*
> *Dustine Edward Marsden Fog,*
> *Captain, Texas Light Cavalry."*

Laying down his pen, Dusty looked at the letter before him and wondered if he could have expressed himself any better, or maybe lessened the blow of having to tell parents that their son would never come back from the War. A feeling of anger and frustration hit him at the thought. How the hell could one soften such a blow? However, he knew that he must write the letter. Hating the task bitterly, he still did it to the best of his ability and, although he never learned of it, his letters did in some small measure help the grieving parents.

Seven letters lay on the table before him, six of them already sealed in the addressed envelopes ready for dispatch. One of the letters bulked larger than the rest. Belle Boyd had written to the parents of the corporal who gave his life for her and added her condolences to Dusty's message.

Coming to his feet, Dusty stretched himself and grunted as his muscles protested at the strain. However, his young frame had become hardened to strain and he felt refreshed by a long night's sleep. Actually it had been closer to a full evening, night and morning's sleep, for he went to bed as soon as he completed cleaning and reassembling his Colts and did not waken until almost nine in the morning. A bath and shave, although that latter had not yet become a daily necessity in his case, refreshed him. After eating breakfast alone in the dining room, the rest of the officers already being about their duty, Dusty returned to his room on the upper floor and set to work at writing his reports and the letters to his dead men's parents.

Like any outdoorsman, Dusty hated to be cooped up in a room. Having completed his paper-work, he decided to take a stroll around the camp. He wanted to see Belle Boyd and discuss the assignment, but he also wished to make sure that his men were all right and that the horses received correct care and attention.

A faint smile flickered across his face as he took up the jacket, now cleaned, pressed and with the metal work gleaming, from where it hung behind the door. His striker, a man with some thirty years' army service behind him, looked ominous and muttered about the *Manual of Dress Regulations* every time he handled the skirtless jacket. In fact, since a certain Lieutenant Mark Counter, something of a Beau Brummel although a man of considerable courage and ability, introduced the skirtless jacket which became popular with the younger bloods of the C.S.A., considerable controversy raged around the propriety of an officer wearing such a garment. The older set, always inclined to damn anything modern, made rumbling noises at the flouting of dress regulations, but many of the younger officers wore and found the jacket comfortable. At that time Dusty and Mark had not yet met,* but the small Texan figured the other to be a shrewd judge of what a *fighting* cavalry officer should wear. The hanging skirt of the regulation jacket was an infernal nuisance and also a serious hazard when forced to make a rapid mount over the rump of a horse, while the skirtless jacket gave greater freedom of movement under all conditions; and, to Dusty's way of thinking, looked even smarter than the old style.

Dusty and Red shared a room on the upper floor of the building, although expecting to be evicted to live with the other junior officers in the tented lines if senior members of the C.S.A. came on an extended visit. Knowing that Dusty needed rest, Red had left early and not returned. So Dusty donned his jacket ready to go out in search of his second-in-command.

Swinging his gunbelt around his waist, Dusty fastened the buckle and then secured the thongs which held the holster tips down. He took up the two Colts. Checked that each nipple had a percussion cap firmly seated upon it and that the hammer of each gun rested on a safety notch between two of the nipples. Taking precautions like that came naturally to Dusty. He knew that even in his regiment's camp he might need his guns, and if he did need them, there would be no time to start checking on and replacing any percussion caps not in place. Making sure the Colts' hammers rode safely was another simple, but necessary precaution. No man with any brains in his head carried a loaded revolver with its hammer resting on a capped nipple.

The door of the room opened and Dusty's striker entered, having heard his officer moving about and guessing

*Dusty and Mark's first meeting is recorded in THE YSABEL KID by J. T. Edson.

that the letter-writing session had ended. Knowing Dusty's views on writing, the striker kept out of the way until the distasteful business had been concluded.

"Take the letters to the orderly room, Dick," Dusty ordered.

"Yo!" the striker answered. "And don't you go tearing about neither. Take it easy for a spell. That danged company of your'n won't fall apart if you leave it for a spell."

"You know it, and I know it," Dusty grinned, "but I don't want Uncle Devil to know it or I'll be looking for a fresh command."

"Hope it's one where they make you wear the right jacket," sniffed the striker, sealing the last envelope and taking up the others.

"If they do, I'm going home to mother." Dusty told his striker and left the room before the other could make any adequate reply.

Dusty walked from the house and made his way through the neat tented lines to his company's area. Visiting Billy Jack's quarters, he heard his sergeant-major's report on the welfare of his men. From there Dusty and the lean non-com passed on to the horse lines where the regiment veterinarian and stables sergeant waited. After checking that the welfare of his horses was well in hand, Dusty gave Billy Jack the good news. Relief showed on the lean sergeant-major's face as he heard that the company would be able to relax and reform before making any more sorties against the Yankees.

"Red and I are going on an assignment," Dusty went on. "Only if anybody asks, we're on furlough. Pappy'll be running the Company until I get back."

"That'll be all right," Billy Jack answered. "If there's no more, Cap'n Dusty, it's Saturday and I've a card game waiting."

"Gambling'll be your downfall," Dusty warned.

Grinning, the lean non-com saluted and ambled away. Dusty watched the other go and smiled. There went a real good man, one in whom a feller could trust his life. Turning, Dusty walked towards the big house. To get there he had to pass a large storehouse which had been emptied and converted into a fencing school for the Regiment. Hearing the unmistakable sound of swords in action, he walked towards the open door of the building and looked inside.

A fencing match was in progress, watched by the *maitre d'armes* and seven or so of the younger officers of the Regiment. Remaining outside, Dusty studied the contestants and noted the high standard of skill both showed. The skill did not surprise him really, for Major Amesley, the *maitre d'armes*—he also acted as the Regiment's adjutant —had been a fencing instructor in New Orleans, and taught the junior officers all he could. Pete Blaze, Red's older brother, could claim to be the best sabre fighter in the Regiment and, although using an *epee de salle* instead of the *arme blanche* of the cavalry, performed with skill. So did his opponent. Clad in her Union army kepi, dark blue shirt, black breeches and light shoes, Belle Boyd handled her *epee* to such effect that Pete could not make a hit on her. Nor could she get through to him. Suddenly she jerked off her kepi, tossed it into Pete's face and went into a lunge. Blinded by the hat, Pete failed to recover in time and he felt the *epee's* button touch him in the belly.

"I always say if you can't lick 'em, trick 'em," Bell stated, avoiding Amesley's accusing eye.

Laughing, the rest of the officers gathered around the girl. Not having been reared under the strict rules of the *code duello*, they regarded the girl's breach of fencing etiquette as amusing. Requests to try a few passes against Belle came from all sides, but as the girl was about to accept one challenge she saw Dusty enter the building. One of the others turned to look at the new arrival.

"Hey, Dusty," he greeted. "Come on in and give Belle a whirl. This gal's a living wonder with an *epee*."

Eagerly the other officers joined in the appeal for Dusty to try his hand in a bout with the girl. Belle regarded the small Texan with expectant eyes and hoped he would agree to face her. Since her arrival at the Regiment's headquarters, she had heard many tales of Dusty's blinding speed and deadly accuracy when using his Colts and also of his ability at unarmed fighting, but little had been said of his knowledge of fencing. She wanted to gauge his ability in that line.

"Loan me an *epee*," Dusty said, "I'll learn how it's done."

Taking the offered *epee* after removing his hat, jacket and gunbelt, he stepped into the centre of the hall. Belle had recovered her hat and moved into place before him, smiling as she studied the relaxed ease with which he handled the *epee*.

A faint smile came to Amesley's face and he moved forward. Nothing could quite compare, in his opinion, to watching the interplay between two skilled users of the *epee*. While he taught the Regiment how to handle their sabres, at heart he clung to the belief that the *epee* was the only true gentleman's weapon and hoped the girl would not spoil what promised to be a fine bout by using any trickery.

Gracefully Belle raised her *epee* in the salute and watched the relaxed, casual manner with which Dusty replied to the courtesy. If the way he handled his *epee* proved anything, he knew at least the basic rudiments of fencing. From what Belle had seen so far among the Texans, that did not surprise her. She wanted to see how much further his knowledge went.

"*En garde!*" Amesley ordered. "Engage."

The blade touched and Belle attacked with a covered thrust but felt Dusty's *epee* deflect her own slightly and parried his counter-attack with a deft wrist twist which gladdened Amesley's heart as he watched. While the opening moves told Belle that Dusty knew more than a little about handling an *epee*, before many seconds passed Belle began to realize just how good he was with that weapon. Yet for all his skill, Dusty found that the girl could handle his attacks and prevented him from making a hit on her.

Steel glinted, hissed and clashed as the bout went on. Attacks on arm and body, thrusts at low or high angulation, *froisse* attacks, *prises de fer,* were made and parried; even beats at the blade, most difficult of all moves to accomplish with an *epee* were tried without the one attempting the beat taking the point of the blade so far out of line that it left the forearm uncovered for a counter thrust. Even the stern old master, Amesley, could not resist joining in the applause when Belle, in the course of her attack, carried her left foot as far back as possible, dropped her left hand to the floor while extending her right arm with the hand high and thumb downward so as to direct her sword towards Dusty in the low line. Only by a very rapid retreat did Dusty avoid being taken by Belle's *passata sotto* and her low lunge, a classic and entirely legal move, carried her body under his blade.

For over a minute the duel went on fast and furiously. Sweat trickled down Belle's face and she had never found a moment when she might chance getting off balance to repeat the trick which beat Pete Blaze. However, she saw her chance as they came in close. Just as Dusty wondered if he ought to call off the contest, for the girl had already taken on Pete in a long bout, he caught a warning glint in her eyes.

Up drove Belle's left foot, aimed at his middle. She gave only that one very faint hint of her plan, but against a man with Dusty's lightning fast reactions such a hint was enough. From the raised balance position, Dusty's left hand sped down and his fingers closed on her leg before the foot reached him. Belle gave a startled yelp as she felt his strength. Then he twisted on the ankle, turning the foot inward and raising it higher than Belle meant it to go. This caused Belle to turn her body away from him and, losing her *epee,* she went down to land on her hands, face to the floor. Still gripping the ankle in his hand, Dusty, placed his right foot between her legs and dropped to his knee so as to bend the trapped limb across his. This move came so swiftly that Belle could not even think of countering it. Pain knifed into her knee and she gasped. Instantly Dusty released his hold and came to his feet.

"I'm sorry, Belle," he said, bending to help her rise. "I just went on with the move without thinking."

A wry smile came to Belle's face. "Mike was right. I wouldn't have fooled you with my *savate.*"

"You sure can handle a sword," Dusty commented.

"I had a good teacher," Belle replied and in an attempt to make amends for spoiling Amesley's enjoyment of the bout by her attempt at trickery, went on, "almost as good as the man who taught you."

"I'd like to see you matched against Dusty when you are fresh, Miss Boyd," Amesley put in, accepting the compliment with a slight bow.

"We'll see what we can do, sir," Dusty promised. "And now, how about coming riding with me, Belle?"

"My pleasure, sir," Belle answered with as near a curtsy as she could manage while slightly winded and wearing breeches instead of a skirt. "If the other gentlemen will excuse me."

Jumping to the wall, Pete Blaze took down one of the *epees* from the rack and returned to block the way to the door. "We won't," he warned. "You'll have to fight your way out."

Eagerly the seven other young officers grabbed training weapons and aligned themselves with Pete.

"Two against eight?" asked Belle with a smile. "How about it, Dusty?"

"Danged if we haven't all but got them outnumbered," Dusty replied and winked at her. "Let's follow the Boyd family motto."

Dropping his *epee,* Dusty went forward in a fast, rolling dive that carried him under the blades of the waiting swords. His hands shot out to grab the inner ankle of the man on either side of Pete and his body struck and knocked his cousin over backwards. Coming erect at the end of his roll, Dusty retained his grip on the ankles, jerking them into the air. Taken by surprise, the trapped men tipped over, to land in a tangled heap upon Pete.

Keeping her *epee* in her hand, Belle bounded forward and into the air in a *savate* leaping high kick. Drawing up her legs, she shot them out, one foot striking each of the central of her four opponents in the chest and flinging them backwards. Rebounding from her attack, which carried her body over their swords, Belle landed on her feet once more. With a swift, deft bound, she twisted the amazed third man's sabre from his grasp. Whirling, Belle lunged at the fourth and passed his guard long before he thought to make it.

"You're dead!" she announced as the *epee* bowed gracefully from hand to chest.

"And so are you, Stan," declared Dusty, scooping up a sabre and delivering a cut at the body of the last of their attackers while that worthy stood open-mouthed and amazed.

Whether any of the eight would have accepted their "deaths" was not to be discovered. A soldier appeared at the door of the building even as Dusty spoke.

"Company A is back!" the man yelled.

Instantly all thought of carrying on with the fun departed and the discomfited attackers untangled themselves to rise and leave the room. Dusty returned his *epee* and sabre to the wall rack, collected his hat, jacket and gunbelt and joined the others outside to watch the returning company.

"Buck's all right," Pete breathed in relief as he watched his twin brother riding at the head of the approaching column.

Leaving his men, Buck Blaze rode towards the others and halted. Although his face showed fatigue, he managed a grin as his eyes rested on Dusty.

"We got it, Dusty," Buck said. "Hardly saw a Yankee all

the way, thanks to you. Prisoner we took at the depot allowed most of the men had been sent west after your boys. You sure riled the Yankees this time out."

"Pleased to hear it," Dusty replied. "Did you lose many men?"

"Four. It'd been a damned sight harder happen you hadn't drawn so many of the Yankee troops to the west."

On a previous attempt at destroying the depot, with less forethought or planning, half a company of a Virginia cavalry regiment were killed or captured. That had been during the period when Ole Devil found himself fully occupied with assuming office as commanding general of the Army of Arkansas.

Dusty watched Buck ride away after Company A. Somehow his cousin's news made him feel better. There had been a big saving of lives through his actions.

"Well, Dusty," Belle remarked after Buck left, "we've fought our way out. Let's take that ride, shall we?"

"I reckon we can," he answered.

Borrowing two horses from the Regiment's remount pool, Belle and Dusty rode from the camp and along the forest-lined trail towards Hope City. At first they talked of Dusty's fighting skills and he described the deadly ju jitsu and karate techniques taught to him by Ole Devil's servant, a smiling Oriental who claimed to hail from some country called Nippon. At last, about a mile from the camp, Dusty brought up the subject which interested him most.

"When do we leave?"

"As soon as authorization to purchase the guns is telegraphed to me from my headquarters. The Government may have some other plans for using the money, or may not want to deal with Smee."

"How'd you figure we'll get to the coast and reach Matamoros?"

"Pick up a riverboat at Fulton and go down the Red, but swing off along the Atchafalaya River instead of joining the Mississippi. Go through Grand Lake to Morgan City and join a fast blockade-runner there, use it to reach Mata-moros."

"And how do we go up the Rio Grande to Matamoros?" asked Dusty. "A Confederate blockade-runner won't be flying the British flag."

"I'm not sure how," Belle admitted. "I think we'll be put ashore south of Matamoros and make our way over-land."

"That'll mean taking horses with us," Dusty remarked.

A red-headed woodpecker flitted from the trees ahead of the horses, made a rapid change of direction and sped off towards the thick bushes flanking the other side of the trail. Then it seemed to be trying to halt in mid-air and its chat-tering cry burst loud as it swung away from the bushes to speed off and disappear into the trees again.

Watching the bird's appearance, Dusty followed its flight until it made the second hurried change of direction. His eyes caught a sight of something blue in colour and at odds with the greens or browns of the surrounding bushes. In a flickering blur of movement, his left hand crossed to draw the right side Colt.

"Come out with your hands raised high!" he ordered, cocking the Colt. "Do it slow and real easy."

Belle halted her horse and for once just sat staring in-stead of reacting with her usual speed. While she carried her Dance in an open-topped holster, she had never mas-tered the knack of drawing it really fast. So far little pub-licity had been given to the deadly techniques of the Western gun fighter and few people in the more pampered East had any conception of just how swiftly a frontier-trained man could draw his weapon. To Belle, who had been engaged in her own business and failed to see Dusty shoot the Dragoon at the mouth of the Funnel, it seemed that the Army Colt just appeared in Dusty's left hand; and for no reason that she could discern.

Hands in the air and moving slowly, a bearded man stepped from the bushes. He had the appearance of a poorer class manual worker and did not appear to be armed. Although blue, his shirt was a lighter shade than that worn by the Yankee army; which was fortunate for him, as Dusty would have shot without challenging otherwise.

"Don't shoot, sir," he said. "Maybe the lady knows what comes after 'Southrons, hear your country call you'."

"Up, lest worse than death befall you," Belle answered. "He's a friend, Dusty. You won't need your gun."

"*My* friends don't hide out when they see me coming," Dusty commented.

"*Mine* do," Belle countered. "Do you have a message for me?"

"Yes, ma'am," the man answered, throwing a glance at Dusty and making no attempt to pass on the message.

"Will you wait here, please, Dusty?" asked Belle, knowing that the man did not wish to speak in front of the small Texan.

"It's your deal," Dusty replied.

Belle and the man walked up the trail, the girl sitting her horse and leaning down to speak. A few moments passed and Belle turned her horse to ride back towards Dusty while the man disappeared into the bushes. Even before Belle reached him, Dusty knew something troubled her.

"We'd better go back to the camp, Dusty," she said. "I've just had some disturbing news."

## CHAPTER EIGHT

# Promotion for Major Amesley

The short, smiling Oriental servant showed Belle and Dusty into Ole Devil Hardin's office. Seated at his desk, the General shoved aside a pile of papers on which he had been working and then came to his feet.

"You wish to see me, Miss Boyd?" he asked.

"I do, General," Belle replied.

"Was just going to send for you anyway. Your authorization to take the money and buy the arms has just come in."

Belle and Dusty exchanged glances and despite their being accustomed to living in danger, both felt a faint tingle of anticipation run through them.

"Give Miss Boyd a chair, Tommy," Ole Devil ordered, for, despite his inborn objections to a young lady wearing men's clothing and indulging in such an unfeminine business as spying, he never forgot the social graces. When the girl had been seated at the desk, he continued, "What did you want to see me about, Miss Boyd?"

"I can't go into details such as who the man was, or how he came by his information, of course," Belle answered, "but I can assure you that the word he brought is genuine and accurate."

"Maybe you'd better tell me which man you refer to," growled the General.

Quickly Belle told of the meeting with the agent and Ole Devil sat stiff-backed in his chair, taking in every word. Moving on silent feet, Tommy Okasi handed his employer a cigar and rasped a match for it. Through the smoke, Ole Devil studied Belle's face.

"The gist of the message is that one of Pinkerton's best men has been on my trail almost ever since I landed in New York. Strogoff, the agent, arrived in Russelville on the day after the gold raid. He investigated it and is sure that I was responsible for it. More than that, my information is that the Yankees guess at the use to which we intend to put the gold—and where."

For the first time Belle saw Dusty and Ole Devil come close to showing emotion. A flicker of expression crossed Ole Devil's face, almost mirrored by the glint that appeared in Dusty's eyes. Watching them, Belle saw how Dusty reacted in much the same manner as his uncle and realized that the small young Texan tried to model himself on the tall, grim-faced warrior who commanded him.

"How the hell did they learn about the Matamoros?" Dusty asked when Ole Devil failed to raise the point.

"Pinkerton runs an efficient organization; never sell him or his men short on that," Belle warned. "I was probably under observation most of the time I was in England. If so, they know about my meetings with Smee, and he isn't the most loyal of men."

"Do you think this Smee jasper sold you out?" growled Ole Devil.

"It's possible," Belle admitted.

"That's not going to make our work any easier," Dusty remarked.

"I know. The U.S. Secret Service don't like Rose Greenhow or me, we've made them look like fools too many times. Pinkerton's crowd swore they would get me after I escaped from the Old Capitol Prison after they put me there."

"I never did learn how you pulled that," Dusty said.

"Some other time, Dustine," Ole Devil ordered and looked at Belle. "In the face of what you've told me, I think you had best stay in the South. Dustine and Red— Damn it, Dustine, you've got *me* calling him 'Red' now—Anyhow, they can make the purchase and delivery."

"I'm afraid that's not so easy, General," Belle smiled. "Dusty and Red are both good fighting men, but they haven't played *my* game long enough to know it."

"How do you mean?" asked Ole Devil.

"I'm not selling Dusty or Red short on any counts," Belle assured him, noting the anger-furrow which came between his eyes. "But you wouldn't send one of your companies out under the command of a civilian—would you?"

From what she had already seen of Ole Devil, Belle figured that line would be the one he understood the best. Her judgment proved correct and an admiring glint crept into the hard black eyes as Ole Devil sat back in his chair.

"I see now how you've stayed alive so long, Miss Boyd," he stated.

Dusty frowned and put his doubts to words. "Belle's a valuable spy and the South needs her, sir." His eyes turned to Belle and he went on, "and I'm not saying that just because you're a woman. But the Pinkerton bunch want you and I've heard they aren't particular how they go about getting somebody they're after. You'll be mighty conspicuous down there."

"I agree, Miss Boyd," Ole Devil put in. "Even though you're a pretty fair hand at disguising yourself, any American girl down there will stick out like a nigger on a snowdrift. Unless you plan to go there as a Mexican."

"My Spanish is non-existent," Belle smiled. "There are some white girls down there, working in the *cantinas* or on the streets, but going as one of them would limit my usefulness."

"Yes," agreed Ole Devil. "There'd be too many places in Matamoros closed to that kind of woman; and I wouldn't want you to go into the kind of hell-holes there are in Matamoros."

"I can take care of myself pretty well, General," Belle replied. "But a *cantina* worker would not serve my purpose."

"We're assuming that the Yankees in Matamoros hear that we're coming," Dusty reminded the others.

"I've told you that Pinkerton's crowd are thorough," Belle answered. "Strogoff had already telegraphed news of the raid to Washington. From there, word can be passed to New York and a fast Navy boat sent off. Even starting today, we could hardly be in Matamoros before word reaches the Yankee spies there."

"We'll lose nothing by assuming that's already happened, Dustine," Ole Devil pointed out.

"Yes, sir," Dusty answered in a disinterested manner which drew Ole Devil's eyes sharply towards him.

Seeing that Dusty did not intend to say more, and knowing his nephew *very* well, Ole Devil turned back to Belle. "Could you pass yourself off as a French girl?"

"Possibly, although my French is of the Creole variety. There can't be so many French girls in Matamoros that the sudden appearance of another would go unnoticed. Of course, it is a thought."

Glancing at Dusty, Belle waited for him to make a comment, but he sat back in his chair, a blank expression on his face. For almost a minute nobody spoke. Then Dusty sat forward in his chair. While he tried to keep his features free from expression, a faint glint of eagerness showed on them.

"What is it, Dustine?" asked Ole Devil.

"Just a fool notion, sir."

"Go ahead," the General ordered, thinking of other occasions on which Dusty came out with a "fool notion" that proved to be a very sound piece of planning and brought success.

"Like we figure, Belle's arrival in Matamoros is bound to attract some attention—no matter what she wears or how she tries to hide."

"We'd already assumed *that*," growled Ole Devil.

"Then why hide her at all? Let her arrive in plain view and with conspicuous company."

"Such as?" asked Belle.

"Let her go into town as the wife, or *amie*—is that the word I want?—"

"It'll do," grunted Ole Devil. "I have heard of even Confederate officers having such things."

"But why would a Confederate officer be in Matamoros?" smiled Belle.

"He could have come in from Texas on an official visit to the French authorities, to discuss—"

Dusty's voice trailed off at that point, for he had not been able to think of a convincing reason for the visit.

"He's come to discuss an exchange of deserters. Quite a few French soldiers have gone over the hill, jumped the Rio Grande and settled in Texas. There are some of our own down below the border. The visit could be to arrange for an exchange—with more serious undertones, such as a closer association between our Government and the French."

"That's a really good idea, General," Belle breathed. "The French would be only too pleased to give us co-operation if they thought their cause in Mexico might benefit by it."

"Only it won't work," Ole Devil answered.

"Why not, sir?" asked Dusty.

"Such a mission would not be handled by a captain, no matter how distinguished his record, and a first lieutenant."

"That's true enough," Belle agreed. "But I still like the idea."

"We need a field, or staff officer with us, sir," Dusty stated.

"I could appoint you temporary rank, Dustine, but you're too young."

"Yes, sir. But it sounds like the kind of trip Pappy would like."

"You know I can't spare an active officer," Ole Devil pointed out. "I can't spare you and R—Mr. Blaze if it comes to that."

Although Ole Devil held the Yankees in Arkansas and had inflicted some heavy losses on them, he did so by superior tactics and fighting ability. Outnumbered by the enemy, only keeping every man fully employed prevented the Confederate Army from being swept back to the borders of Texas and held them firm beyond the Ouachita. Taking Dusty's company out of the field would mean cancelling, or postponing several projects as Ole Devil well knew. He could not spare both Hondo and Dusty at one time.

"Major Amesley could come, sir," Dusty suggested. "His orderly room staff do most of his work anyway, and he's champing on the bit to see some action."

"You could be right at that," smiled Ole Devil. "Wouldn't need to put too much strain on his leg and he's got the way with him to carry the affair off."

"There would be no objection on age grounds to Major Amesley receiving promotion, General," Belle remarked.

"How do you mean, ma'am?" asked Ole Devil. "You think I should appoint him a lieutenant or full colonel for the trip?"

"A brigadier general would be even better," she replied calmly.

"A *general!*" Ole Devil barked.

"Yes. The French Army officers are either members of the *ancien regime,* or, as they say, of the people. The former respect a man for his breeding, which we know the Major has, and his rank. The latter, like most of their type, are arrant snobs and are more likely to show deference to a general that to a major or colonel. One other point to remember is that a general would be more likely than a colonel to have a captain and first lieutenant on his staff."

"That's true," conceded Ole Devil, then smiled. "So's everything you said. However, promotion from major to brigadier general might be construed as straining the powers of even the commanding general of the Army of Arkansas."

"My department would back you on it," Belle promised. "Put it down to the necessity of the situation. And the promotion would only be temporary—and unpaid."

"You can be certain of the last," Ole Devil informed her definitely.

"And all the expenses will be defrayed from the Yankee gold," she went on.

"I should think so too," he replied, and for a moment his face softened in a smile.

In that moment Belle saw the kindly man hidden under the hard mask of discipline and façade of irascible nature. The mask did not stay broken for long and the old, cold face returned.

"My compliments to Major Amesley, Dustine," he said. "Ask him to come to see me as soon as it's convenient. Which means right now, convenient or not."

"Yo!" Dusty replied, rising and crossing to the door.

Five minutes later, Dusty returned with Major Amesley at his side. For the first time Belle noticed the slight limp which told that the wound received in the early days of the War had left its mark. While waiting for Amesley to appear, Ole Devil had told the girl how the major received the wound and also mentioned his age. Belle could hardly believe that tanned, sprightly man had sixty years on his shoulders and would have put his age at the most in the very early fifties.

Emotion played on Amesley's face, although only one who knew him as well as did Ole Devil Hardin could have noticed it, as he approached the general's desk. Being a well-educated man, Amesley could easily add together two and two to make the correct answer. He knew Belle's identity and guessed that something important kept her in the area. Nor had Dusty's excitement—again only observable to one who knew the signs—gone unnoticed. Amesley hoped against hope that the call to Ole Devil's office meant a chance to get away from dull routine and perform some useful fighting task for his country. The old wound stiffened his leg to the point where continued strenuous exercise rendered it unable to move with the speed necessary to keep a combat soldier alive. So he did duty as adjutant and trained the young bloods to handle their swords, much as the tasks galled him. Watching Ole Devil, Amesley prayed that there would be a change in the air.

"Sit down, Beau," Ole Devil said, waving a hand towards the chair Tommy Okasi brought to him. "Do you know the Mexican port of Matamoros?"

"Can't say I do, sir."

Ole Devil proceeded to run through the situation, with Amesley listening attentively and casting occasional glances at Belle or Dusty. At the end, he nodded his head.

"I can handle my part of it, sir," he stated.

"Well, be cagey with it," Ole Devil warned. "Nobody in our Government will come out with a definite official statement about siding either the French or the Mexicans, not wanting to antagonize either side. You'll probably find the French brass mighty interested. Particularly those so close to the border. Feel them out, learn all you can about their sentiments, but don't make any promises that our Government will have to stand by or refute later."

"May I say something, sir?" Dusty put in.

"Feel free," Ole Devil answered.

"The Yankees are going to be real interested in our reason for being in Matamoros."

"I'd say so."

"And they'll probably put it down to our trying to organize an alliance with the French."

"Probably."

"Then they'll be watching us all the time."

"No, Dustine," Belle interrupted. "They'll be watching 'General' Amesley. He has to hold their attention and leave you and I free to arrange for the shipment of arms when Smee arrives."

"That may be," Dusty replied doubtfully. "But while the Yankees are watching Major Amesley, they're going to see him spending a whole load of their gold."

"So?" asked Ole Devil.

"Aren't they going to think that just a little mite strange? A Confederate 'General' spending Yankee gold."

"I think I can answer that, General," Belle stated. "Going from what I saw in Europe—and I can't see Mata-moros being any different—there'll be considerable reluctance to accept paper money issued by either side."

"That figures," Ole Devil answered. "Whichever side wins won't uphold the other's currency. Foreigners would fight shy of taking something that may wind up by being just so much paper after the end of the War."

"Then you don't reckon the Yankees'll be suspicious when they see us spending U.S. minted coins?"

"Not if we use coins with pre-war dates on them," Belle asserted.

"Are any of the coins dated before the War?" asked Ole Devil.

Nobody replied for a moment, then Dusty looked across the desk. "I don't reckon any of us thought to look, sir," he admitted.

"Then somebody had better look," growled Ole Devil. "And soon."

"I'll see to it, sir," Dusty promised. "Sure hope that it's all in double eagles though, or I'll be checking it all day."

"You've maybe got something better to do?" asked Ole

Devil with a grin, then turned his attention to the rest of the occupants of the room. "Anything more before we break this off, Miss Boyd?"

"I'd like somebody to arrange our passage down river," Belle answered.

"Have your orderly room sergeant see to it, Beau. Have you anything you want?"

"Only my stars and sleeve insignia," Amesley replied. "How about my staff?"

"You'll have Dustine and Red Blaze as your aides and Miss Boyd will be your *amie*. I'll leave it to you how you arrange *that*."

"Servants, sir?" Amesley continued.

No Confederate general would travel without at least one servant to minister to his needs and all present knew that everything must appear normal if their mission was to succeed.

"Any suggestions, Dustine?" asked Ole Devil.

"My striker, he's a cool hand and can be trusted to keep his mouth shut. And I reckon Billy Jack'd go to private to act as Major Amesley's striker."

"A brigadier general could run to a sergeant-major for striker, sergeant at least," Old Devil countered. "But why Billy Jack?"

"Dick's a mite long in the tooth for rough games and this might turn out to be real rough," Dusty replied. "Anyways it's time Billy Jack had a furlough."

"Will he volunteer to go along?" Belle inquired.

"I'll order him to volunteer," grinned Dusty. "How about a maid for you?"

"We'd best hire one down there, say mine quit before we left Texas," Belle answered.

"Which brings up another point," Dusty went on. "You'll be travelling as a lady—"

"Why thank you 'most to death, kind sir," smiled Belle.

"You know what I mean," Dusty answered. "That means you can't ride into Matamoros dressed like you are today. Which also means that you going in afork a horse is out."

"Well, Dustine?" queried Ole Devil.

"We need a carriage of some kind, sir. And we can't hope to be lucky enough to pick one up on some deserted bay on the Mexican coast."

"Take one with you," Ole Devil suggested. "Pick it up either in Alexandria or Morgan City. You'll need something to carry the gold on and pack horses wouldn't be the best answer."

Watching the men, Belle was struck by the attention they paid to small details. Many Army men she knew would never have thought to discuss the matter, but send her out to fend for herself. Belle felt gratified and pleased with the way her luck placed her in the way of such helpful and competent men.

"Anything more?" asked Ole Devil.

"Only how we're going to handle the transportation of the money, and I reckon I can handle that, sir," Dusty answered.

"Miss Boyd?" Ole Devil went on.

"Nothing that I can think of off-hand."

"Beau?"

"I'll take up anything I think of with Dusty, sir."

"Then that's all, Miss Boyd, gentlemen."

Rising, Dusty and Amesley saluted their general and left the office with Belle on their heels. At the door Amesley halted and looked down at his sleeves.

"Brigadier General," he smiled. "Now there's a promotion for you, Dusty."

"Yes, sir, General," Dusty answered, grinning back. "It sure is—even if you don't get paid for the rank."

## CHAPTER NINE

## Captain Fog Encounters
a Travel Hazard

Before the War, the *Rosebud* had made the big run along
the Mississippi from St. Louis to New Orleans and completed for trade with the many other side-wheeler steam-
boats which carried passengers and freight at speeds no
other form of transport could equal. However, the War
disrupted the river-boat trade, for the Yankees controlled
the Mississippi's lower reaches and their gunboats raided
far up-stream in a manner which rendered peaceful trading
decidedly risky. Only a few of the boats remained in business and the *Rosebud* found a useful route lay between
Fulton on the Red River in Arkansas and Morgan City
down at the mouth of the Atchafalaya.

What with shortages of freight and passengers, word
that a brigadier general, his niece—being a man of the
world, Captain Boynes of the *Rosebud* accepted that the
young woman accompanying "General" Amesley *might* be
his niece—and staff wished to make the full trip was
something of a windfall. In accordance with the *Rosebud*'s

tradition of hospitality and luxury, Boynes and his clerk
stood on the boiler deck at the point where the double
stairway from the main deck curved together, and waited to
greet their distinguished passenger. There were no boilers
on the "boiler" deck, it being given over to the big main
cabin which served as lounge, dining room, bar and general gathering place for the first class passengers. Lining
the main cabin on its two outer sides were the passengers'
accommodation; known as staterooms due to the early-day
practice of naming each room after a State of the Union.
Each stateroom had one door opening into the lounge and
another gave access to the promenade-deck which surrounded the superstructure.

The *Rosebud*'s reputation for luxury and good service
had been honestly made and even with the War in progress
some of the old standards remained. Stewards in clean
white clothing darted along the main deck to collect and
carry the newly arrived party's baggage aboard and to the
boiler deck. At one side the mate stood glowering at the
delay and waiting to set his roustabouts to work at preparing to haul in the gangplank and cast off.

"Who is this General Amesley, Rube?" Boynes asked of
his clerk, a man with an almost encyclopaedic knowledge
of who was who in Arkansas.

"Never heard of him, Cap'n. Them buff facings on his
uniform mean he's in either the Adjutant General, Quarter-
master General Commissary or Engineer's Department. A
desk-warmer most likely."

"Those two with him aren't desk warmers though,"
Boynes stated, nodding to Dusty and Red as they followed
Belle and Amesley up the stairs. "That's the Texas Light
Cavalry uniform and arms belts."

After some discussion at Regimental headquarters it had
been decided that Amesley travelled down to the coast in
his new rank so as to become accustomed to answering to
his temporary title of "general"; a minor consideration
some folks might have thought, but Belle insisted on it and

Ole Devil backed up her superior knowledge of the deadly game they played. They must take no chances, for the Yankee spy organization did not employ fools and a mistake might ruin the entire assignment. Again following Belle's recommendations, the Regimental tailors had worked all night to remove the cavalry yellow stripes from the legs of Amesley's trousers and replace them with the double row of buff-coloured cloth as became a general officer of one of the non-combatant departments—all generals wore buff facings on their jackets no matter to which branch of the Army they belonged.

Using her knowledge, Belle suggested that Amesley posed as a member of the Adjutant General's Department. Being concerned with the legal aspects of the Army's organization, such an officer would be the most likely choice to handle negotiations for the exchange and return of deserters. In addition, the Adjutant General's Department rarely came into the public's eye, which would explain why Amesley's name was not familiar to any Yankee spy. Finally, a member of the non-combatant Adjutant General's Department on such a mission might be expected to have along a couple of combat soldiers as his escort; which explained away Dusty and Red's presence.

Stepping forward, Boynes raised a hand to the peak of his hat. "Pleased to have you aboard, General," he said. "My clerk here will escort you to the Number One stateroom."

"Thank you, sir," Amesley replied. "And what of my staff?"

"Your niece is in the next stateroom, the captain and lieutenant beyond her and I've put your strikers in a cabin on the Texas deck."

"My thanks, sir," boomed Amesley. "Come along, Clarissa, my dear."

"Will there be any danger from the Yankees, Cap'n?" Belle asked.

Only it was not the calm, competent Belle Boyd who

organized the raid on the Dragoons' camp and helped plan the present assignment; but a fluttery, naïve, not too bright young thing just asking for a big, strong man to protect her. The change went far beyond merely donning a stylish travelling dress—purchased in Hope the previous evening —hat, blonde wig and parasol. If Dusty had not known the real Belle, he would have taken her for what she pretended to be. Certainly the *Rosebud*'s captain did not doubt her character.

"Land-sakes no, ma'am," he answered, glowing with protective manhood. "You'll be as safe aboard the *Rosebud* as if you were at home. Now if you'll excuse me, I have to get us under way."

"If you'll come this way, General Amesley, sir," the clerk said, bowing and waving a hand towards the double doors of the lounge.

Although the stewards handled most of the baggage, Dusty and Red insisted on carrying their own saddles. Each of them had his range-rig slung over one shoulder and a Henry rifle swung in his other hand. Dusty decided to take along the fifteen-shot Henrys rather than the Spencer carbines so as to have extra fire-power should it become necessary to make a fight.

The other passengers, Army officers going on furlough, civilians travelling about their business, and a few women, studied the new arrivals with varying degrees of interest. Taking in the buff facings and leg stripes, the Army men knew Amesley belonged to a non-combatant department; they also noticed the fine *epee de combat* which hung in his belt slings instead of the usual general officer's sword. Nor did the soldiers fail to observe his fighting man's carriage and decided that his slight limp prevented him from commanding a fighting outfit.

"At ease, gentlemen," Amesley said, breathing a little easier as he looked around and failed to see anyone who might recognize him as the adjutant of the Texas Light Cavalry.

While Amesley might go unrecognized, the same did not apply to Dusty and Red.

"I tell you that's Captain Fog," an infantry major said to the artillery officer at his side as they watched Amesley being escorted to the best stateroom on the boat. "I saw him lead a charge at Mark's Hill that turned the course of the battle."

"Him?" scoffed the other. "That small kid—"

"He didn't look small to me and my company that day," the major growled.

Other eyes studied Dusty and Red. A couple of young lieutenants from the major's regiment exchanged glances.

"Texas Light Cavalry," one said. "Look at those gun-belts. They must think they pickle their nuts in salt-brine."

"And those damned Yankee rifles that you can load on Sunday and shoot all the week," the second answered. "I wonder if they've any ammunition for them, or if they just tote them to look big."

"We'll see before we reach Shreveport," grinned the first. "Wonder what they're doing going down the river?"

"On furlough most likely. Who's the general?"

"Some shiny-butt from back east most likely. Reckon we'll meet him later."

"We'll meet those two horse-soldiers while we're at it," staked the second.

Fortunately for their future well-being, the *Rosebud* started moving before the two shavetails managed to meet Dusty and Red with the object of proving an infantryman's superiority over the cavalry. Just as fortunate, the infantry officers met their major and learned Dusty's identity before the small Texan made another appearance in public.

While comfortable, Dusty and Red's stateroom could not be described as spacious. It contained a couple of narrow, though well-padded bunks, a washstand and a small, curtained-off area just large enough to hang a few clothes in. When the two saddles and the bulky pouches carrying spare clothing and ammunition had been laid on the floor, little space remained for walking about the room. Being hardened veterans, even though so young, neither Dusty nor Red worried unduly about their surroundings. Both had lived considerably rougher than at present during their time in the Army.

"Let's go see how the others are getting on," Dusty suggested after the boat churned away from the Fulton docks.

After visiting Belle and Amesley, and finding both settled in comfortably, Dusty and Red went up one of the flights of stairs leading to the Texas deck. This perched on top of the boiler deck and, in addition to housing second class passengers, the senior members of the boat's crew, clerk's office and barber's shop, offered a larger area than the promenade deck below on which travellers might take exercise. Set on top of the Texas deck was the wheelhouse, its large glass windows offering the pilot and captain an unrestricted view of the river and surrounding country.

Dusty and Red did not go up to the wheelhouse deck, figuring that the pilot and captain would not want visitors underfoot at that time. Instead their attention was drawn to a small bunch of the younger passengers who gathered at the rear of the Texas deck cabins to watch a display of pistol shooting. The shooter, a tall, slim, well-dressed young man in civilian clothing, held a magnificent percussion-fired single-shot duelling pistol in each hand. Taking sight with his right-hand weapon, he fired and severed the neck of an empty bottle standing on the guard rail at the end of the deck.

Moving forward, the Texans saw a pretty, stylishly-attired young woman with the two infantry shavetails.

"Of course, my brother wanted to join the Army," she was telling the officers, her voice warm, friendly and inviting. "But the Government asked him to continue running the family business. We manufacture firearms, you know. You, being service officers, can imagine how he felt about that."

"A man has to do his duty where he must, Miss Dimsdale," the taller shavetail replied, although he might not have taken so lenient and tolerant a view of an able-bodied man who failed to answer the country's call to arms if the man did not possess such a charming sister.

"Poor Paul," the girl sighed. "He's such a fine shot and a wizard with a sword. He would have made a good soldier. As it is—well, you must be our guests at dinner tonight."

"We'd be right proud to, Miss Dimsdale," agreed the second officer.

While listening to the by-play between the girl and officers, Dusty and Red paid little attention to it, being more interested in the shooting. As good shots themselves, Dusty and Red could admire another skilled performer, and the slim civilian proved to be all of that. At twenty-five feet the neck of a bottle did not make a large target, even when armed with the ultimate of handgun precision, a duelling pistol.

"He's some shot," Red remarked as the second bottle's neck burst under the impact of a bullet. "Those are straight-shooting guns, too. I reckon you can take him though, Dusty."

"Well, don't you go flapping off your mouth about it," Dusty answered.

At that moment Belle appeared on the deck and walked along to join the two Texans. Although she still looked as when she boarded the *Rosebud,* Belle sounded her old, competent self.

"I heard the shooting," she remarked in a low voice, her eyes going to the good looking girl who still stood with the two officers.

"There's nothing to worry about," Red replied with a grin.

Again Belle threw a glance towards the other girl. "Isn't there?"

Glancing at Belle Dusty wondered what she had seen to

put a burr under her saddle. He knew Belle too well to put the dislike she showed towards the other girl down as mere feminine jealousy and hoped she would enlighten him. Before Belle could do so, Captain Boynes came down from the wheel-house deck, saw his most important passenger's "niece" and strolled over to greet her. Instantly Belle reverted to her new character and Dusty did not find an opportunity to ask her about her dislike.

Time dragged by, with the *Rosebud* continuing to make good speed with the Red River's current pushing under her and aiding the turning of the big side-wheels. Dusty and Red found little chance to speak with either Belle or Amesley alone all day, but being interested in the novelty of their new surroundings did not let that worry them. Night came and the dinner gong drew passengers to the main lounge. Amesley was joining a party of senior officers at the captain's table but Belle came to sit with the two Texans. Even with the War on, the *Rosebud* offered a very good menu, although much of the meat would be from wild animals rather than beef.

"Brother Buck and brother Pete never had it this good," Red stated.

Thinking back to the antics Red's brothers brought off on her final night with the Texas Light Cavalry, Belle smiled. "Buck and Pete don't deserve it this good," she declared, then turned her head to look across the room as a burst of laughter rose from a table where the two infantry officers sat with the Dimsdales. "Now there's a couple of young men looking for trouble."

"A lot of folk entertain soldiers these days," Dusty answered. "Folks who wouldn't look at a man in uniform other times get all friendly when the shooting starts."

"You're a cynic, Dusty," Belle smiled. "And I've a suspicious mind. I *could* be doing those two an injustice, but I doubt it. Did you ever hear of a firearms company called Dimsdale?"

"Nope—not that that means anything. There're a lot of small companies making arms for us on contract to the bigger concerns."

"Reckon they're Yankee spies, Belle?" Red asked when Dusty stopped speaking.

A faint smile crept across Belle's face. "I doubt if they're anything as dramatic as that. Look at the 'General'. He appears to be enjoying his new rank."

Realizing that Belle had said all she meant to on the subject of the Dimsdales, Dusty and Red turned their attention to eating. Almost three years' service in the Army had given them a fatalistic outlook and they now tended to live for the moment. So, given an opportunity like at the moment, they always ate well; a man never knew when he would be on short rations.

Through the meal Belle watched the Dimsdales' party and noticed that while the soldiers drank frequently neither their host nor his sister attempted to keep up with their consumption. Once the meal ended, Belle found herself the centre of a party of young officers and reverted to the part she played, which prevented her from being able to pass on her theories to the Texans.

Never really happy in a crowd of older men who held lower rank than themselves, Dusty and Red backed out of the group surrounding Belle and went out on to the deck. Deciding to make the most of their opportunity while aboard the *Rosebud*, Dusty and Red strolled around the promenade deck and then went down the stairs to the bows of the main deck. Up forward, on either side of the bows, an iron cresset held a brightly glowing fire of knotty pine chunks and the flames illuminated some of the river's surface and left side shore line. In times of peace there would have been far more cargo stacked foward, but the War had an adverse effect on trade. However, a few large packing cases lined the sides and one very large box stood up in the bows, a clear passage running through the rest of the cargo to it.

Behind the cargo came a storage of cut wood ready for use and then lay the furnaces, boilers and engines which drove the paddlewheels and propelled the *Rosebud* through the water. Coloured firemen fed the flames of the furnaces and the engineer, a bulky, grimy-faced white man, supervised everything. At the stern, the Negro roustabouts threw dice, talked, or slept in the knowledge that they had no more work to do until they reached the next town.

Although not a man who encouraged passengers to loaf around his domain the engineer raised no objections in Dusty's case. Having heard the small Texan's name, the engineer decided that a young man with such a reputation for fighting Yankees had earned the right to be treated as an equal. Leaving his post for a time knowing he could rely on his crew of firemen, the engineer greeted the Texans. The War was discussed, with much profanity on the engineer's part. Then a question from Red brought the subject around to riverboat work. Sitting on the rail so he could keep an eye on the working of his engines, the engineer began to talk about the good days before the War when the *Rosebud* ran the Mississippi. He told of wrecks, explosions of boilers due to over-pressure, races and cargoes which almost set the decks awash with their bulk and weight. For a man who punctuated almost every sentence with blistering invective, the engineer painted a vivid picture of life on the riverboats. At last, after mentioning river pirates, he turned to the fabulous gambling for which the boats had become notorious. Listening to the latter reminiscences, Dusty began to see the reason for Belle's suspicions of the Dimsdales.

"Don't get so much of it now, though," the engineer concluded. "Folks don't tote that much money with 'em. Not that we ever had much on the *Rosebud*. Cap'n Boynes stopped it when he could."

At that moment Red pointed ahead, along the side of the boat and towards the illuminated shore. "Whooee, Cousin Dusty. Look there!"

Turning, Dusty followed the direction of his cousin's pointing finger. A low whistle of admiration left the small Texan's lips at what he saw. Standing at the edge of the water, its head thrown back proudly and its great spread of antlers rising high, as fine a bull elk as Dusty had ever seen stood watching them. Then it gave a quick, explosive snort, whirled and bounded off into the blackness beyond the fire's glow.

"See a lot of 'em," remarked the engineer. "Deer, bear, cougar even. The old *Rosebud* don't scare 'em until she gets real close. Happen you feel like sport, bring a couple of rifles down here some night."

"I never took to shooting something just to see it fall," Dusty replied. "Nor me," admitted the engineer, "But happen you shoot anything, we can put off one of the boats we're towing and the roustabouts'll fetch it aboard. The cook can use the meat."

"We'll see about it," Dusty promised.

"Well, I'll be getting back to work," the engineer said.

"Sure. I reckon we'll go back to the lounge, don't you, Cousin Red?"

"I'm ready when you are," Red agreed.

On their return to the lounge, Dusty and Red felt amazed to discover they had been away for over two hours. Several card games were in progress, including one in which Amesley played oblivious of distractions. Dusty saw that Dimsdale sat at a table in the middle of the lounge and close to the passage which led between two staterooms and on to the promenade deck. Watched by his sister, Dimsdale played twenty-card stud poker with the two officers and a bluff, hearty-looking man who wore the dress of a prosperous farmer. Dusty saw that although the girl kept the soldiers supplied with drinks, she treated her brother and the farmer less generously.

Standing with a couple of young artillery officers, Belle was in a position to keep her eye on the game. Catching

Dusty's attention, Belle excused herself and moved around the Dimsdales' table to meet him.

"It looks straight enough so far, Dusty," she said in a low voice.

"How's it going?" he replied.

"Evenly so far, no exceptional wins or losses. I could be wrong about them. Do you know the game?"

Dusty nodded. Twenty-card stud, with only the aces down to tens of each suit used, had a reputation for being a real fast gambling game. Each of the four players received his first card face down and bet blind on it, then played with the remainder of the cards face up. With so few cards and every one in play, a man needed a clear mind to follow the game correctly and it needed following if one wished to avoid substantial losses. From what Dusty could see, liquor had dulled the two soldiers' judgment.

"You say that they're not losing much?" he asked.

"Not yet," Belle answered.

At that moment the Dimsdale girl yawned, in a ladylike manner, and stirred uneasily in her chair. Turning, her brother smiled at her. "Tired, honey?"

"A little. Will you be long, Paul?"

"How about it gentlemen, will we?"

"I don't want to keep a *lady* from her bed, Paul," the farmer replied, laying great emphasis on the word "lady".

Drunk they might be, but the two young officers were Southern gentlemen and raised in a tradition of chivalry towards the opposite sex.

"Nor me," the taller declared.

"We'll finish now," his companion went on. "Unless you want to chance playing without Miss Maudie sat there to bring you luck, Paul."

"Oh, I'll be all right, gentlemen," Maudie cooed.

"No, ma'am," the taller shavetail insisted, reaching towards his money. "We're calling the game off right now."

"Just have one more hand," Maudie suggested quickly

—maybe a shade too quickly the listening Dusty thought, and a glance at Belle told him her mind ran on the same general lines.

Both soldiers appeared to be reluctant to keep Maudie any longer from her bed and Dimsdale shrugged. "All right. Hey, though, it's my turn to buy the drinks. One more hand while we drink them, then win or lose we break up the game for the night."

"I'll go and fetch them," Maudie suggested. "I need to walk, my—limbs—are stiff from sitting so long."

Before any of the men could comment on the propriety of a young lady doing such a menial thing as fetching a tray of drinks, the girl rose and walked towards the bar. Handing the deck to the taller soldier, Dimsdale requested that he prepare to deal.

"Give 'em a real good riffle this time, Jefferson," the farmer suggested with a grin. "I've not seen a good hand all night."

Taking the cards, the soldier started to give them a thorough riffle. However the farmer interrupted the game to tell a story and the riffling continued after the joke's conclusion. Maudie came towards the table, a tray of drinks in her hands, as the soldier set the deck down before the farmer to be cut. In doing so, Maudie had to pass where Belle stood in apparently earnest conversation with Dusty.

"Why I tell you-all, Captain Fog," Belle said, "that Simmerton girl wore a hat with a brim this size—"

And to illustrate her point, Belle spread her arms wide apart. In doing so, the left slapped upwards under the edge of Maudie's tray and knocked it from her grasp. Tray, glasses, liquor, all went tipping into the air and drew every eye in the room towards the noise. However, most people's attention went not to the tray or the enraged face of Maudie as whiskey spread over her dress—but to a deck of cards, identical to those in use at her brother's table, that fluttered out of the girl's fingers which had held them concealed under the tray.

## CHAPTER TEN

## Miss Boyd Arouses Suspicions

A silence that might almost be felt dropped upon the room at the sight of the cards and knowledge of their implications.

"Your—sister—dropped something, *hombre*," Dusty remarked.

Dimsdale's eyes went to the scattered cards, then lifted to Dusty's face. Snarling out a curse, the man started to thrust back his chair and rise. His right hand moved towards his left sleeve's cuff—and froze inches from the concealed butt of a Derringer pistol as he found himself looking into the barrel of Dusty's left-hand Colt. Never had Dimsdale seen such speed and he could hardly believe that he looked into the .44 calibre muzzle of the long barrelled revolver which less than a second before rested in its holster at Dusty's right side.

Although not as fast as his illustrious cousin, Red took the farmer out of the game as that worthy began to rise and reach in the direction of his inside pocket. Twisting his right-hand palm out, Red closed his fingers around the butt of his off-side Colt and slid it from leather to end such hostile moves and gestures.

"Now just sit there easy, *hombre*," Red ordered and the click of his gun coming to full cock added force to his words.

Leaving the card game he played with the senior officers, Boynes crossed the lounge fast. "That's a whole lot of card for a game of stud," he said. "Reckon this is where you asked to get off, Mr. Dimsdale."

"I don't know what you mean," Dimsdale answered suddenly.

"You want for me to search your baggage?" countered Boynes.

Knowing that such a search would produce even more damning evidence against him, and cause the loss of a lot of gambling equipment of a highly specialized nature, Dimsdale surrendered.

"We'd like to be put ashore here," he gritted through his teeth.

Turning to the gaping infantrymen, Boynes asked, "Did you lose much?"

"I'm a hundred down," the taller replied. "Say, did he —were they—"

"Sit down, mister!" Dusty barked as the soldier began to rise and, despite the amount of liquor the infantryman held, he knew better than to disobey.

"You boys split out what's on the table between you," Boynes suggested and Dimsdale raised no objections.

All the time the men spoke, Maudie had been glaring with almost animal fury at Belle. "You caused all this!" she screeched and threw herself at the Southron girl with fingers crooked ready to grab her.

Not wishing to show her talents in the art of self-defence before the passengers, Belle retreated hurriedly and backed down the passage towards the door to the promenade deck. She kept ahead of and clear from Maudie's fingers, thrust open the door with her rump and backed out. Still shouting unladylike curses, Maudie followed and the door swung closed behind her. Nobody moved, the fury on Maudie's face had been enough to halt the men. A crack like two billiard balls connecting sounded on the promenade deck. The door burst inwards and Maudie entered, moving backwards. Spinning around, she hit first one wall then the other before falling into the lounge and landing face down upon its floor. A moment later Belle appeared, looking the same naïve, fluttery blonde.

"Oh my!" she gasped, looking down at Maudie's recumbent body with well-simulated horror. "The door swung back and hit her. I *do* hope she isn't hurt."

Possibly only Dusty and Boynes had been in a position to see what happened along the passage and neither of them intended to mention that the door had closed *behind* Maudie before the crack of fist against chin sounded.

Watched over by the mate and Red Blaze, Dimsdale and the "farmer" stood at the side of the lounge while Boynes examined the cards. Not that he needed any further proof than the presence of the second deck. However, he found the deck in use on the table to be marked.

"It's an old game," he told Dusty. "The gambler lets his victims hold their own most of the evening, then rings in a cold deck by some trick. This time the girl would have held the tray out so it hid the deck on the table and the farmer would have made the switch unseen. Then the officer, believing it to be the deck he riffled, deals out good hands, the betting is forced up, and either Dimsdale or the farmer wins it. That way, if the victims don't want to play the next night, the sharp has made some profit."

"What'll you do with them?" Dusty asked.

"Put them ashore. They know what to expect."

"Not the girl," Dusty objected, nodding to where Maudie sat on the floor, holding her jaw and with tears trickling down her face.

"She was in on it," Boynes growled.

Having been raised with a belief that no man could meet with a worse fate than being set afoot, Dusty pleaded for the girl. He spared no sympathy for the men, but stated frankly that he would not countenance the girl being put ashore and forced to walk the fifty or more miles to the next town.

"Have it your way," Boynes grinned. "Take those two to the main deck, Mr. Hogan, and see that they go ashore as soon as possible."

"Aye, aye, sir!" boomed the mate. "Let's have yez, buckoes. Make one wrong move and I'll be busting your hands."

"No rough stuff, friend," Dimsdale purred. Then his eyes went to where Dusty and Belle stood watching him. Shrewd judge of human character though he might be, the gambler could not decide whether Belle's intervention had been pure accident or done deliberately and with knowledge of the forthcoming switching-in of the cold deck. Then his eyes went to Dusty again and saw a real *big* man. "Maybe we'll meet again some time, Captain Fog."

"Maybe," Dusty replied.

"Let's go," the mate ordered, and the gamblers passed out of the lounge.

Crossing to where Maudie rose, Baynes ordered her to go to her stateroom and stay in it until they reached the next town. Obediently Maudie left the lounge and from that moment maintained silence on what happened when she followed Belle through the promenade deck door. Maudie had her pride and hated to think that a feather-brained girl like the blonde could flatten her with such ease. Not until much later did Maudie start to wonder if maybe that blonde hadn't been quite so naïve as she pretended. Naïve or not, the blonde certainly knew how to throw a punch. It was a long time before the aching throb left Maudie's jaw.

While Maudie retained her silence about the attack, at least one person in the lounge felt very interested in the way she came to make such a dramatic re-entrance. Events brought every game of cards in the room to a halt, including one involving three field rank army officers and a trio of civilians; only one of whom is of any interest. Manny Engels, plump, prosperous-looking, sat staring across the room and trying to reconcile Belle's handling of Maudie with what he had seen of her so far. After giving Belle's face a long, searching glance, Engels dropped his eyes to the recumbent Maudie, swivelled them to where Dusty stood covering Dimsdale and finally turned his gaze to Belle once more. In the silence which followed the dramatic happenings, Engels heard Belle's explanation for Maudie's condition, but he did not find it convincing. There was more to the affair than met the eye, Engels felt sure of that.

"Let's get on with the game, shall we?" asked one of the players as the gamblers left the room.

"Deal me out," Engels replied. "I'm tired and want to take a turn around the promenade deck before I turn in for the night."

None of the other players raised any objections, so he collected his money and left the table. On the promenade deck, he walked along until he could see the two gamblers and their baggage put ashore. However, after the boat started moving again, he did not follow his proposed course of going to bed. Instead he found a shadowy corner of the deck and remained in hiding. Time dragged by, but Engels showed patience. At last a light glowed in one of the staterooms as its lamp was brightened. A moment later he saw Dusty Fog emerge from the next room, walk along the deck, take a stealthy, cautious look around and then enter the newly-lit door.

On silent feet Engels moved towards the stateroom. Apart from Captain Boynes, nobody on the *Rosebud* knew of Dusty and Red's connection with Amesley and Belle. If any of the other passengers thought of the matter at all, they assumed that the Texans were grabbing an opportunity to make a trip down-river while on a furlough. However, during the trip, Engels had noticed that Belle spent some time in private conversation with Dusty and showed reluctance to be seen doing so. Being of an inquiring nature, Engels decided that the matter might prove worth investigating. A clandestine association between a junior officer and the *amie* of a general—Engels discounted the idea of her being Amesley's niece—offered possibilities handled properly.

On silent feet Engels advanced towards the door of Belle's stateroom and cocked his head towards it, listening to the conversation within. Due to the nature of its design and construction, the upper portions of a riverboat were of necessity made of light and flimsy material. Being thin, the walls of the stateroom allowed Engels to listen without approaching too close.

"That was close, Dusty," Belle remarked as the small Texan slipped into her room through the promenade door shortly after she entered from the lounge after pleading that the excitement had given her a headache.

"Sure was, Belle," Dusty agreed. "Happen she'd laid hold of that wig, the folks would have thought she'd hand-scalped you."

"Likely," Belle answered and smiled as she realized how she now slipped into using the laconic terms her Texas friends employed. "I don't think anybody was on the promenade deck to see me hit her as she came through the door. She did look surprised when I stopped and let her have it."

"Yeah," Dusty drawled and, keeping his voice at the same easy drawl, made his way cautiously towards the promenade deck door. "I wonder what the folks in the lounge are making of it?"

Even as he spoke, Dusty twisted the handle of the door and wrenched it open. Fast though Dusty had moved, Engels licked him to it. On the first movement of the door's knob, Engels started to walk away along the deck. Although he had not gone far, the man put himself beyond any chance of Dusty proving that he had been eavesdropping on a private conversation.

"What was it?" Belle asked, joining Dusty at the door.

"I'm not sure," Dusty replied. "Just got the feeling that somebody was out there, but he'd passed by when I got the door open."

"Do you think he was listening?"

"I don't know. Reckon he might have been though."

"Do you recognize him?" the girl asked.

"It's a travelling man, seen him around the boat, but I don't know his name."

"We'd best stay away from each other until he leaves the boat," Belle suggested. "And I'll keep my eyes on him."

"Be best. You know this game better than I do," Dusty agreed. "I'll get out of here while there's nobody watching. If any of the womenfolk aboard see me leaving your stateroom it might cause talk."

"Not only women gossip," Belle smiled.

"Nope," Dusty replied. "But they do more of it than we do."

With that Dusty stepped through the door and walked along the promenade deck. Smiling still, Belle closed the door behind him and went to prepare for bed.

Engels continued his stroll around the deck, guessing that Dusty watched him. Showing no sign that he had been listening, he turned the corner of the promenade deck and circled around until he reached his own stateroom. Inside, he started to undress and while removing his shirt came to a sudden halt. One of the necessities of a man in his line of work was the ability to remember conversations, and he turned the words he had heard over in his mind. Why had the Texan addressed the girl as "Belle," and what did the reference to her wig mean? When Engels first saw Belle, he marked her down as the beautiful but brainless *amie* of an elderly man. Now he wondered if there might be something deeper than that about the blonde beauty.

Sitting on his bunk, and leaving his undressing as thoughts began to churn through his head, Engels tried to remember if he had ever heard of a General Amesley. No such name came to his mind, although he felt inclined to put the fact down to Amesley belonging to the non-combatant Adjutant General's Department—or had been inclined to think that at first. Maybe Amesley only pretended to be on the Adjutant General's staff. Perhaps he held an appointment in another Department which tried to keep its activities out of the public's eye. Amesley might be one of the powers of the South's efficient Secret Service. In which case the girl most probably was not Amesley's *amie*.

Belle! The name bounced back into Engels' mind almost as if powered by a blinding light. When one thought of the Confederate States' Secret Service and heard the name Belle, one immediately coupled the name with Boyd. Excitement ripped into Engels at the thought. Belle Boyd; one of the South's top two female spies. If the girl on the boat should be Belle Boyd, that accounted for why she wore a wig. Never had such important information come Engels' way and he hoped he could make the most of his discovery. He wondered if he might learn what mission took Belle Boyd and Captain Dusty Fog down the Red River. Being aware of Dusty's reputation and having a fair idea of Ole Devil's shortage of men, Engels knew only a matter of the greatest importance would take the Texan from the firing line. Discovering the nature of the assignment could greatly add to the profit his information about Belle Boyd brought in.

With the idea of confirming his suspicions in mind, Engels entered the lounge at breakfast time the following morning and looked for the objects of his interest. Belle and Amesley shared their table with a couple of the top-class families while Dusty and Red sat among the younger officers. In passing, Engels halted at Belle's side and, in the pretence of inquiring after her health after the excitement of the previous evening, studied the girl. Sharp though he might be, he saw nothing in her answer or appearance to suggest that she might be other than what she appeared on the surface. Although he studied it carefully, he could find no proof that the neatly coiffured blonde curls might be a wig. However, he did notice a change in Amesley's attitude towards Belle. The "General" now showed some interest in Belle that had been lacking the previous day. After seeing Engels bedded down for the night, Dusty had visited Amesley and warned that they might be under observation, offering the suggestion that more interest in his "niece" might not come amiss.

During the remainder of the trip down to Shreveport, Engels continued his surveillance of the party. After some thought, he decided that Red might prove the most fruitful of the quartet to pump. However, Red had been primed for such a move and his answer told Engels only that he and Dusty had taken a furlough and aimed to see what pleasures Alexandria or Morgan City might offer. Nothing Engels learned from Red gave any hint that other than a pleasure trip brought the two Texans from Arkansas. However, Engels learned, from hints Red dropped, that the two young men travelled as Amesley's aides so that their expenses might be defrayed against the taxpayer, the "General" being an old friend of the family and not averse to doing a good turn for an influential person like Ole Devil Hardin.

On the second night Engels kept a close watch, but saw nothing to help him. Dusty and Red spent the early part of the evening on the main deck, where Red's Henry rifle brought down a prime young whitetail deer buck which would be of use to the boat's cook. After that the Texans returned to the lounge where they joined the other young officers in a rowdy, low-stake game of *Vingt-Un*. Amesley and Belle spent their evening in the company of the senior passengers and Engels decided to keep watch in case of another visit by Dusty to the girl's cabin.

In stateroom after stateroom the lamps were extinguished and Engels stayed patiently in his position at the stern end of the promenade deck. Midnight came and just as the man decided he would go to his room, he heard a door open along the deck. The promenade deck was illuminated by a couple of small lamps and Engels could see that Amesley, not Dusty Fog left his room and entered the girl's quarters. Stealthily the watcher moved forward and halted outside the door of Belle's stateroom. He heard only what one might expect from such a visitation and after a short time decided that his suspicions might have been wrong. Assuming that nothing further would happen that night, Engels went to his bed. He did not know that while he watched Amesley, Dusty kept an eye on him; nor that after his departure Amesley returned to his own stateroom to spend the night.

"What do you think, Dusty," asked Belle, as they met while strolling on the hurricane deck the next morning.

"He watched you last night," Dusty replied, leaning on the protective rail and watching the shore slip by. "I don't know if we've got him fooled or not. Seeing a Confederate "General" go into your cabin wearing just his shirt, pants and socks ought to have convinced him."

"If he heard what we said, it could," Belle said, and smiled in recollection of an incident in her cabin. "Poor Major Amesley looked real embarrassed at entering a lady's room that way. He—I sure won't be sorry to get to Morgan City, Captain Fog. I do declare this itty-bitty cabin's plumb ruinous—Oh, good morning, Mr. Engels. How are you-all on this beautiful morning?"

In a flash, on seeing Engels approach, Belle Boyd disappeared to be replaced by Clarissa, Amesley's "niece". Having seen the girl in earnest conversation with Dusty, he attempted to get close enough to hear what was being said; but Belle proved too quick for him.

After making small talk with Dusty and the girl for a time, Engels passed on. Nor had he reached any decision when the boat pulled into Shreveport. Watching Maudie Dimsdale take her departure, Engels decided that he might possibly learn something of use from her. He knew the boat would not be departing for two hours at the least and so went ashore. Following Maudie, Engels found no difficulty in striking up an acquaintance. Her "brother" had left the *Rosebud* without providing any money for her well-being and over a meal she told Engels what had happened when she followed Belle out on the promenade deck.

While listening to the girl's description of how an amazing change came over the blonde, turning her from a scared little milk-sop to a cold, deadly female who used her fist like she knew what it had been given her for, Engels happened to look around the room. A feeling of cold shock hit him as he saw a tall, gangling sergeant-major of the Texas Light Cavalry seated at a nearby table and apparently engrossed in eating a meal.

Engels felt sure that the "blonde" on the boat must really be Belle Boyd, and also guessed that she and her escort must be suspicious of him. Slipping some money under the table to Maudie, Engels made the usual suggestion and she agreed.

"I'll just have to go out back first," he told the girl and thrust back his chair. "Wait for me."

While walking towards the door marked "MEN'S," he figured she would have a long wait.

CHAPTER ELEVEN

## The Inventive Genius of Mr. Henry and Captain Williams

"And there I was, just a-sitting and waiting," Billy Jack admitted as he stood on the hurricane deck of the *Rosebud* with Dusty. "Comes fifteen minutes, I got to figuring that happen it took him *that* long, he should be told how good croton oil works. So I went to tell him and, dog-my-cats, if there's not another door out of the room. It led to the street, but time I got 'round to figuring *that*, he'd up and was long gone."

Looking at his sergeant-major's miserable expression, Dusty had difficulty in holding down a grin. Billy Jack knew Dusty's attitude when somebody reported a failure through lack of foresight, and expected an explosion. However, Dusty realized that the lean non-com had not been trained in the business of following a suspected person and so made a mistake which lost Engels.

"It can't be helped," Dusty declared. "I'll go down and see if he's come back on board."

"You reckon he's a Yankee spy, Cap'n Dusty?" asked Billy Jack.

"I'm keeping an open mind," Dusty answered. "He did meet up with that Maudie gal and buy her a meal. But that doesn't mean he wanted to learn anything from her."

"Nope," agreed Billy Jack. "Happen he's come back, what say we lay hold of him tonight and ask him a few questions?"

"He might not want to answer," Dusty pointed out.

"Maybe he'd change his mind after he'd been dragged head down for a spell behind the boat."

Unfortunately for Billy Jack's plan, one essential item was missing. On visiting the clerk's office, Dusty learned that Engels had sent a messenger to the boat with instructions to collect his baggage. Knowing that travelling salesmen often made unscheduled departures should business come their way, the clerk raised no objections and could offer no suggestion as to where the baggage went after leaving the boat. Nor did he connect Engels' departure with a letter brought aboard for delivery to an address in Alexandria; although both the baggage collector and the man who brought the letter had been hired by the departed Engels.

While Dusty would have liked to make an immediate start to search for Engels, the *Rosebud* was due to leave Shreveport before he could do so. Allowing Billy Jack to return to the card game which went on pretty continuously in the barber's shop, Dusty went down to the boiler deck and located Belle, Red and Amesley.

"Billy Jack lost him," Dusty told them after making sure he would not be overheard by any of the passengers other than his party. "He followed Engels into town and saw him meet up with that Maudie girl. Engels took the gal into an eating house, bought her a meal and then started talking quiet to her. She did some answering but Billy Jack couldn't hear what they were saying."

"Could have been asking her what happened on the

promenade deck," Amesley commented. "Most likely was; if he's a Yankee spy and suspicious of Miss Boyd."

"Reckon he is a Yankee spy, Dusty?" asked Red.

"Could be. Or maybe he's just the kind of sneak who'd listen at a stateroom door for fun."

"The riverboats have always been good sources of information." Belle put in. "A solider going on or coming off furlough tends to talk more than when he's with his outfit. There's a chance that Engels was aboard to learn anything he could."

"What'll we do about him?" Red growled.

"There's not much we can do," Belle replied. "We can't delay our trip while we go back and look for him. Even if we could persuade Captain Boynes to turn around without telling him far too much. When we reach Alexandria, I'll see a friend and arrange for a very close watch to be kept on Mr. Engels."

"Happens he's decided that you aren't what you seem, maybe even guessed that you're Belle Boyd," Dusty said quietly. "Can he pass on the news to the Yankees?"

"I'd be surprised if he couldn't," Belle answered. "There's no telegraph to them, of course, but he could pass the message verbally, or written and concealed on a courier."

"Which same the feller couldn't reach the Yankees until long too late to find us," Red stated, sounding a mixture of relief and disappointment. Red always craved for excitement and had so far found the trip boring.

"Unless Engels decided his information is so important that he sends it by carrier-pigeon," Belle warned.

"Do you reckon he might do that?" Amesley inquired. "Would he have access to the pigeons, I mean?"

"Don't sell the U.S. Secret Service short, Major," Belle replied. "I'd bet that every major town along the river has its spy set-up including pigeons hid away somewhere."

"Of course it could be that we're blowing this thing up out of all proportion," Amesley said. "Engels might be no more than a venal sneak who wanted to know something bad about a young man who's gained the fame he can never achieve. The kind of man who's a failure himself and wants to bring everybody down to his level."

"We *could* hope for that, sir," Dusty admitted. "But I'd hate like hell to rely on it. I figure we should work on the assumption that Engels is a spy and that he'll send word about us to the Yankees on the lower Mississippi."

"And what will they do?" asked Amesley.

"Was I the Yankee commander, I'd make a stab at stopping us," Dusty stated. "Reckon they could do it, Belle?"

"I'm not sure," she replied. "Why not go ask Captain Boynes? He knows the river better than any of us."

The men adopted Belle's suggestion and took their problem for solution to Captain Boynes. Having seen his boat safely on her way out of the harbour, the Captain welcomed "General" Amesley and Dusty to the wheelhouse deck. Amesley followed the plan arranged as they came up to the topmost deck, by explaining that he was on an important mission with Dusty as his escort. Without going into too much detail, Amesley went on to say that he feared the Yankees might make an attempt to intercept him and prevent his arrival at Morgan City.

"What're their chances of doing it, Captain?" Dusty asked when Amesley finished speaking.

"How do you mean?" Boynes inquired.

"Could the U.S. Navy's Mississippi Squadron get through and attack the *Rosebud?*"

"With their iron-clads or gunboats?"

"Something like that."

A grin came to Boynes' lips. "The Yankees might control the lower river, but we own everything for a good way below the Atchafalaya. We've batteries of guns that nothing short of a full-scale battle *might* break through. And if there's a sign of a break-through, there's a fast sidewheeler kept fuelled and ready to run up river like the devil after a yearling to raise the alarm."

"How about them slipping through at night?" Dusty went on.

"Not with iron-clads or gunboats. Going upstream they'd have to use their engines, which means noise and flames glowing from their smoke-stacks."

"Could they run through in one of those submarine things I've heard about?" Amesley wanted to know. "We've used them and I reckon the Yankees could have them."

"Maybe they have," admitted Boynes. "But the biggest only carried six or eight men."

"That'd be enough if they got in close and planted their explosives," Dusty pointed out.

"They'd have to get close enough to do it," Boynes answered. "Even underwater that'd take some doing. Don't forget that my pilot's used to spotting things under the river's surface even in the darkness. If he could see a snag* in floodwater mud, he'd not miss anything as large as a submarine."

That figured as Dusty admitted to himself when thinking of the skill every successful river pilot must possess if he hoped to keep his boat out of danger.

"There's nothing to worry about then," Amesley commented.

"Not too much," Boynes agreed. "But I'll make sure that we keep an extra careful watch, General."

"My thanks, sir. And, of course, I don't need to ask you not to mention my mission to anybody."

"You don't," Boynes replied. "I don't want my other passengers worrying, and they sure as hell would if I let them know about your mission."

Returning to the boiler deck, Amesley found Belle surrounded by a bunch of junior officers. A scowl from the "General" caused a hurried scattering of the shavetails and

* Snag: Tree which has fallen into the river and is embedded in the bottom.

Amesley sat at the girl's side to tell her of the meeting with Boynes.

"We don't have much to worry about then," she said. "I didn't expect any trouble until we're beyond Alexandria anyway. Of course, we may have nothing to fear even then."

While Belle did not sound any too certain as she spoke she would have been even less so had she been in a position to see a carrier-pigeon rise from the wooded country about a mile to the east of Shreveport. Circling twice until it got its bearings, the bird struck off in a south-easterly direction, headed down river in the direction of Yankee-held territory.

The journey went on without incident. Mile after mile fell behind the *Rosebud* and Dusty's party settled down to the tedium of travelling. Each night Dusty and Red took their Henry rifles to the main deck where they kept watch for some suitable addition to the boat's larder.

On arrival at Alexandria, Belle and Dusty went ashore and the girl made arrangements for a watch to be kept on Engels. From the same source she made the arrangements, she learned the latest news concerning her mission. Clearly the Yankee Secret Service knew, or guessed, where the gold taken in Arkansas was going and that meant they would try to stop its arrival. Just how far the Yankees might have gone with their plans Belle could not learn. While hoping for the best, she prepared to handle the worst.

After loading up a good-sized cargo of cotton which would be run through the Yankee blockade and sold in Europe to help finance the Confederate war effort, the *Rosebud* pulled out of Alexandria on the final leg of its journey to the town of Morgan City.

"There's not much chance of getting anything tonight, Cap'n Dusty," said the mate, Hogan, as he stood at Dusty's side. "This's 'gator country."

Earlier that day, the *Rosebud* had left the main river to

follow the narrower but still navigable reaches of the Atchafalaya. Thick wooded country closed in on either bank,
ideal territory for animals had it not been for the menace of
the big Mississippi alligators which Dusty had seen
sprawling on sandbars or diving hurriedly from the banks
as the boat approached. Living in fear of alligator attacks
made the local game far more alert, watchful and suspicious than the creatures of the upper river. However, the
cook needed meat, so Dusty and Red had agreed to try
their luck that night.

Accompanied by the mate and the pilot's cub—assis-
tant—the two Texans stood partially concealed behind the
big wooden crate which still rested forward in the bows
and clear of the piles of cotton bales which now covered
most of the free space on the main deck. The cressets
glowed brightly, lighting the river ahead and flickering
upon the shoreline at both sides, giving the waiting men a
clear sight of any animal which might be risking the
dangers by coming to the river's edge for a drink.

"We'll give it a bit longer," Dusty stated.

Time dragged by slowly and the men scanned the banks
for any sign of life. Up in the wheelhouse, the pilot stood
at the big wheel and his eyes never left the dull ribbon
which glowed ahead as what little light filtered down from
above reflected on the river's surface. Long practice had
trained him to look beyond the area illuminated by the
cressets and pierce the blackness of the night in a never-
ending search for signs of danger ahead.

"Capn!" he said.

Turning from the door of the wheelhouse where he had
been standing and talking with a few passengers, Boynes
stepped to the pilot's side.

"What's up, Marse?"

"Up ahead there," the pilot answered. "I saw the loom
of some—Yes. There it is. By cracky! It's—"

He stopped speaking and his right hand stabbed up to
close on the whistle's cord, jerk at it and send a series of

piercing blasts ripping through the night.

At about the same moment that the pilot called to Boynes, Red Blaze peered along the river, squinted his eyes and then he pointed. "What's that ahead there, Dusty? Up the river."

The rest of the meat-hunting party followed the direction of Red's pointing finger. All could see the dark shapes, blacker than the surrounding area and contrasting with the dull ribbon of water, one near each bank of the river. Being more used to such sights than the Texans, Hogan recognized the dark bulks first; and did not like what he saw.

"Boats!" he growled. "Trouble ahead."

Loud in the night rang a series of blasts from the *Rosebud*'s whistle. In echo to it came a spurt of flame from the right side boat, the crack of exploding powder, and an instant later Dusty felt something strike the side of the *Rosebud* under the level of the main deck. Following the shot from the boat cannon, oars dipped down and tore apart the river's surface as powerful arms propelled two big naval launches forward and on a course to converge with the approaching riverboat.

Raising his leg, Hogan delivered a powerful kick to the big box they had used for cover. It appeared to be of poor construction, for the sides burst open and fell outwards. Grabbing quickly, the pilot's cub caught the falling top of the box and flung it aside. In less time than it took to tell, the box had gone and its contents stood revealed. Mounted on a swivel instead of the usual artillery carriage, a box of ammunition by its side, stood a Williams rapid-fire cannon, its one-pounder barrel pointing ahead.

Dusty and Red might have felt surprised, or delighted, to see such an effective weapon at that moment, but neither had time. Long used to reacting swiftly in an emergency, they wasted no time in idle speculation. That shot meant the approaching boats did not bear welcoming friends and so they took the appropriate action. Two Henry rifles raised swiftly, their butts snuggling against shoulders and their barrels lining on the boats. Trained fingers squeezed triggers and worked loading levers, firing bullets, ejecting empty cases and replacing them with loaded rounds so the cycle could be repeated and a hail of lead sweep into the oncoming boats.

Nor did Hogan and the cub react with any less speed or decision. Jerking open the lid of the ammunition box, the cub took out a self-consuming paper cartridge. The gun already held a charge as was proved by Hogan not operating the mechanism so that loading could take place. Standing behind the gun, he gripped the firing handle with his right hand, while his left took hold of the weapon's reloading crank. Hogan knew that the left-hand launch, not having fired the four-pounder boat cannon in the eye of its bows, offered the greater menace at that moment, so he gave it his attention. Turning the Williams on its swivel, he took sight and his thumb depressed the lever on the side which served as a trigger.

The whip-like crack of the Williams merged with the rapid beating of the two Henry rifles. Muzzle-blast flames stabbed out and a one-pound, 1.75 inch ball tore from the Williams. At so short range, even a light ball could inflict damage on the timbers of a launch. The ball struck the boat just over the water-line, burst through and ripped into the leg of the ensign who prepared to open fire with his own cannon. A scream burst from the young officer's lips. His hands jerked convulsively, one tugging the firing lanyard and the other swinging the gun so it pointed away from the *Rosebud* when it fired. As a result the four-pounder's ball missed the river-boat.

On firing, Hogan twirled forward the cranking handle and the breech opened. The cub dropped in the charge he held and bent to scoop another from the box. Around went the handle, the breech closed and sheared the end from the cartridge to expose the powder to the percussion cap's spurt of flame—said cap being automatically fed on to its nipple from a spring-loaded container. Long before either cannon in the launches could complete the tedious process of muzzle-loading, the Williams fired again and a third time; each ball hammering into the boat.

Voices yelled, women screamed and feet pounded on the boiler and promenade decks as the passengers heard the sounds of the fight. However, the pilot and men on the bows refused to be distracted, knowing that the safety of the boat and all aboard her depended on their attention to duty.

The Yankee attack had been well-planned. Two big launches—each with a crew of twenty men armed with cutlasses and either Navy Colts or Spencer carbines—had come up the Mississippi under oars, slipping by the shore batteries and guard boats during the night. On reaching the point where the Atchafalaya cut off from the main river, the launches turned south and laid in wait for the *Rosebud* to make her appearance. Given surprise and the backing of the four-pounder boat cannon each launch carried, the Yankee force should have been able to sink the big side-wheeler; and might have succeeded but for the alertness of the pilot and Red Blaze—and the inventive genius of Mr. Tyler B. Henry and Captain Williams, C.S.A.

Handled by two men skilled in their use, the Henry rifles caused havoc and confusion out of all proportion to their size. Lead raked the two launches, striking down the men at the oars and throwing the others off their stroke. Equally deadly, perhaps even more so, the Williams added its quota to the rout of the enemy. Time after time, working at almost the full sixty-five rounds per minute maximum speed, the rapid-fire cannon drove its balls into the side of the launch on the left side of the river. As the number of holes grew, so water began to pour into the rocking launch. Then the weight of the cannon took the bows down and the crew plunged into the water.

Caught in the repeated hail from Dusty's Henry, the right-hand launch swerved violently into the path of the approaching *Rosebud*. Swinging the tiller, the coxswain tried to steer his charge out of danger; but he only partially succeeded. The *Rosebud* caught the launch a glancing blow, hesitated for a moment, then the thrust of the paddles drove it on. Jolted by the impact, the nearest cresset tipped over and dumped its flaming contents into the passing launch. Yells rose as the Yankees sailors tried to avoid the downpouring fire. A man, his shirt blazing, screamed and dived into the river. Then the launch capsized and its crew found themselves floundering in the water.

With the safety of his passengers to consider, Boynes did not hesitate in his actions. Behind him men struggled in the water, some wounded and bleeding in a manner likely to attract the attention of any hunting alligator which caught the taste of gore, but he could not stop to render aid. Already some of the attacking party had reached the shore and their metal cartridge carbines cracked. Calmly Boynes dabbed his cheek where glass from a breaking wheelhouse window splintered it and then he rang up full speed ahead. On the main deck, the cursing engineer, riled at missing what sounded like a real good fight, laid hold of the controls and increased the pace of the turning paddle-wheels.

Lowering their hot, smoking rifles Dusty and Red looked back down the river. A few spurts of flame showed where the Yankee sailors on shore took final shots at the departing *Rosebud,* but neither Texan wasted lead in replying.

"That was close," Dusty said.

"Real close," agreed the mate and slapped a hand fondly on the breach of the Williams guns. "But we sure showed them how the old *Rosebud* can fight."

"Wonder what those Yankees were after?" the cub put in.

"Figured to stop this load of cotton getting down to Morgan City," Hogan answered. "What else?"

While Dusty and Red would have given the mate a good

answer to his question, neither offered to do so. The small Texan took one final look back along the river before going to the boiler deck in search of Belle and Amesley.

After passing through a congratulatory crowd, he entered the lounge and went to where Belle stood alone.

"Major Amesley's up with the captain," she explained. "What do you think, Dusty, was the attack by chance?"

"Could be, but I doubt it," he replied. "Anyway, we're through them now."

"We're through the Mississippi Squadron's effort," the girl corrected. "Next time it will be the Yankee Secret Service. I'll bet they're watching for us in Morgan City in case the sailors failed to stop us."

## CHAPTER TWELVE

## Miss Boyd Sees a Snake Fight

Before the War, and the Yankee blockade increased its importance, Morgan City had been such a small place that it hardly rated the second portion of its name. Even now, though vastly grown due to the sudden increase of trade and prosperity, there was little sign of permanent settlement, as the majority of the new buildings appeared to be of a flimsy nature, hurriedly erected and made of whatever materials came to hand.

Although three ocean-going ships lay at the docks or just off-shore in Atchafalaya Bay, the arrival of the riverboat *Rosebud* still drew a crowd of loafers. Mingling with the crowd and looking no different from many of its members, two agents of the U.S. Secret Service gave the approaching *Rosebud* a careful examination.

"Looks like she's seen some fuss," Joe Riegel, tall, heavily built, and dressed like a waterfront idler, remarked, nodding to the raw plug in the cannonball hole under the *Rosebud*'s bows.

"She got through though," Murt Fanning, also tall, lean and wearing cheaply elegant clothes that looked much too good for him, answered.

They watched as the riverboat came alongside the dock, its two side-wheels giving a manoeuvrability no screw-driven vessel her size could equal. Down came the gang-plank with a rush almost as soon as the boat came to a halt. Urged on by a mate, roustabouts darted about their tasks and soon the passengers began to come ashore. In accordance with tradition, the most socially prominent passengers left first. The Yankee spies studied Amesley and Belle as Boynes saw them off his ship.

"Reckon that's her?" Fanning inquired.

"Can't see any other blonde gal with a reb general, can you?"

"Nary a sign. What now?"

"We follow 'em, that's what. Most likely they'll be putting up at the Dixie Plaza, but Flora'll want to know if they don't."

The mention of their superior's name brought a wry twist to Fanning's lips. "Can't say that I go a whole lot on taking orders from a woman."

"You tell it to her then," grinned Riegel. "Only make your will afore you do it. Come on, let's get clear and along the street towards the Plaza."

On leaving the boat, Amesley and Belle waited for Dusty to join them and spent their time saying their good-byes to various people or avoiding invitations to visit. A general, even one in a non-combatant outfit, could expect good service and a two-horse open carriage rolled up, its driver seeking business.

"Have the bags put aboard, Mr. Blaze," Amesley ordered. "We'll go to the hotel and you can follow us with the men."

"Yo!" Red replied, glancing at the crowd and feeling pleased that he would not be responsible for the safe keeping of the money.

While the loading of her and Amesley's baggage went on, Belle sat in the carriage looking about her with interest. Her eyes went to the three ships, passing from one to the next, estimating their readiness for sailing. Not until the bags, with the money hidden in false bottoms, had been safely stowed and the carriage began to move off did she mention her conclusions. She sat at Amesley's side, facing the driver, while Dusty took the opposite seat.

"How well do you know Morgan City?" he asked, keeping his voice low.

"I shipped out of here on my way to Europe," Belle replied. "We're in luck, Dusty, the *Snow Queen*'s in."

"Which ship was that?" Amesley asked.

"The three-masted, screw-propeller craft painted lead-grey, laying off-shore. She's a fast sailer, used to run ice to the south before the War."

A vessel employed in the business of transporting ice from the northern states to countries which never saw snow had need of great speed. Such a quality also was of use to a blockade-runner.

"Will she do for us?" asked Dusty.

"I know her captain. Stacey Millbanks is a loyal Southron and a good man. I wouldn't care to trust the gold aboard the *Dora* and the *South Star*'s only just arrived, she's still taking off her cargo."

"Then it's the *Snow Queen* for us," Amesley stated. "How do we find Captain Millbanks?"

"We'll do it after we've been to the hotel and settled in," Belle replied.

After following Belle's party to the Dixie Plaza Hotel, the two Yankee spies prepared to deliver their information to the controller of the U.S. Secret Service ring in Morgan City. They walked along the main business street of the town and passed through a side alley to enter an area of tents and wooden buildings all devoted in one way or another to entertaining visitors to the city. Set back in a clump of trees, the small house attracted little attention; nor did its owner wish it to, for anybody who wanted to use its amenities could easily learn of its whereabouts and needed no help in finding it.

"Where's Flora?" Fanning asked the bulky man in the loud check suit as he came towards them on their entrance.

"In her office. You don't reckon she'd be laying with one of the sports, now do you?"

Scowling, Fanning shoved by the bouncer and walked across the comfortable lounge. A few scantily-dressed girls who sat around the room gave Fanning and Riegel hardly a glance, for neither were of any use in the business way, being employed, or so the girls imagined, by the madam of the house as touts to steer in customers.

"They've arrived, Flora," Riegel announced. "The *Rosebud* pulled in with a hole in her. It looks like the Mississippi Squadron tried to stop her."

"And failed," Flora hissed, coming to her feet. "Is the girl Belle Boyd?"

"We've never seen her," Fanning pointed out.

"Nor have I, that I know of," Flora said, her voice a low, hate-filled hiss. "But she exposed one of my friends in Richmond and broke up a good spy-ring. I want her stopped, you two. Don't forget, if it's Boyd, she has fifty thousand dollars of our money."

"She's at the Dixie Plaza now," Fanning put in.

"As it's the only decent hotel in this God-forsaken town, she would be," answered Flora. "But she'll be wanting to contact Captain Millbanks as quickly as she can."

"Why Millbanks?" asked Fanning. "There's three boats in—"

"You don't think she'd be fool enough to trust herself and *our* fifty thousand in gold, to Duprez of the *Dora,* and the *South Star* won't be ready to sail for at least three days. No. The *Snow Queen*'s our ship."

"Do we get word to the blockade ships?" asked Riegel.

"And have them bungle it again?" Flora spat out. "No. We settle Boyd here in town. I don't know what she aims to do with that gold, the pigeon message didn't say. But whatever it is, those soldiers will be lost without her. Get rid of Boyd first and the rest will be easy."

"How do we get rid of her?"

"How the hell would I know, Fanning?" Flora spat out. "Watch for a chance. It—Wait though. If I know Millbanks, he'll be at the snake fights all this afternoon. And if I know Boyd, that's where she'll go looking for him. Get over there, you pair. If you can arrange an "accident" to her—do it."

"*Snake*-fights!" Dusty said as he and Belle walked towards where an excited, shouting crowd of men and women gathered at the foot of a slope on the edge of town. "I've seen dog-fights, cock-fights, even bull-fights. But I've never heard of snake-fights before."

"You soon will have," Belle smiled back. "Don't ask me what the fascination of them is, but they're very popular down here." While speaking, she and Dusty mingled with the people surrounding a twenty-foot wide, five-foot deep pit dug in the ground, its sides lined with shiny metal sheets. Pointing to a slim, handsome man in the peaked hat and uniform frockcoat of a sea captain, Belle continued. "There's our man, Dusty."

However, Dusty's attention was riveted on the bottom of the pit, and the two snakes which had just been tipped into it. Harsh and menacing came the warning burr from the big, thick-bodied snake on the far side's tail rattles as it landed in the pit, slithered a few feet and then coiled itself defiantly. Up raised the flat, triangular-looking head, jaws opening to show the hideous fangs and the flickering forked tongue. The big diamond rattlesnake lay in the pit, evil as sin and a whole heap more deadly.

Showing much less caution than when he unloaded the rattlesnake, the promoter of the snake-fights tipped the second contestant into the pit. Four feet long to the diamondback's five and a half, and nowhere as bulky, the

roundheaded, somehow pop-eyed challenger did not appear
to have a chance of survival. For a moment it darted at the
sides of the pit, trying without success to climb the metal-
sheathed walls. Then it became aware of the diamondback's
presence. Instantly it stopped trying to escape. The slim body
curved into an elongated "S" and the small head raised high
as it studied the coiled horror in the centre of the pit.

Silence dropped on the watching crowd. Only the inces-
sant buzz of the rattler's warning call sounded. Wriggling
forward fast, the slim snake avoided a strike by the
diamondback's powerful, poison-backed jaws. Like a flash
the thin body began to curl around the thick, harsh-scaled
length of the other snake. The diamondback began to throw
itself wildly around the pit, thrashing and struggling to
break the steadily-tightening hold laid upon. Again and
again the diamondback slashed and drove its head at the
other. Slowly but surely, the slim snake's coils tightened
and it moved nearer and nearer the spade-shaped, evil
head. From a long tangle the two snakes became a knot,
then a ball of pulsating movement. For almost fifteen minutes the struggle raged, beginning with fast movement and
slowing gradually until at last all movement ceased.

"Well, I'll be damned if that skinny ole snake ain't
killed the rattler," said a soldier at Dusty's side.

"He for sure has," grinned the civilian standing next to
the private. "Reckon that's five dollars you owe me."

A faint grin came to Dusty's face at the words. That
"skinny" killer belong to the *Lampropeltis Getulus* family,
the king snake, which lived exclusively on other snakes,
killing their prey by constriction and to a certain extent
being immune to the other's poison. Apparently the soldier
did not know that in such an affair the king snake almost
invariably won the fight.

Before Dusty could enlighten the soldier, Belle tugged
gently on his arm and led him to where Captain Millbanks
stood holding a wooden box that had small holes drilled
into its top.

"May I speak with you on a business matter, Captain Millbanks, please?" she greeted.

Turning, Millbanks looked first at the girl, a hint of recognition on his face, then he turned his gaze to Dusty for a moment, studied him with eyes which knew how to read a man's true potential.

"I'll be with you after I've settled a small matter here," Millbanks replied.

"Come on, Cap'n Millbanks," one of the nearby men put in. "Let's see what kind of critter you've brung along."

Nodding politely to the girl, Millbanks stepped along to one of the tubs in which the contestants for the fights could be displayed. Cautiously he opened and up-ended the box, shaking its contents out. A low mutter of surprise rose from the onlookers as they saw Millbanks' challenger. Lying coiled passively, the snake appeared to be no more than three feet long and slender, its head smallish and rounded, while bands of alternating black, yellow and red colour ran along its body.

"That sure is one fancy critter," an onlooker remarked and eyed Millbanks. "Can it fight?"

"There's one sure way to find out," he replied. " Drop it in the pit and see."

"Air it pizeness?" inquired another of the crowd.

"Wouldn't want to put my hand in there and see," admitted Millbanks. "But I *will* put my money on this fancy old snake of mine."

While the discussion of the fighting possibilities of the "fancy" snake went on, Riegel and Fanning stood to one side and their eyes went to Belle.

"She went straight to Millbanks," Fanning declared. "Now we know she's Belle Boyd."

"That's right. Now we know," agreed Riegel.

"What do we do?"

"Arrange that accident—and here's how we do it."

Unaware of the danger which threatened her, Belle stood smiling indulgently and watching Millbanks accept wagers on his snake. Despite his insistence that the snake be given odds, due to it never having fought before, she felt that he might not be making any mistake. Few of the crowd thought so, for all knew the deadly poisonous qualities of a diamondback rattlesnake or a copperhead and had seen king snakes emerge victorious from combat with both. Belle did not mind the delay. Having seen the tensions under which a blockade-runner lived at sea, she could hardly begrudge Millbanks some relaxation, even of such a bizarre nature, while ashore.

At last the preliminaries had been taken care of, and some substantial wagers made on the result of the fight. With their money at stake, the gamblers in the crowd insisted on selecting an opponent and decided upon a king snake almost four feet long which had defeated more than one really big rattlesnake or copperhead.

Carefully Millbanks slid his contestant into the pit and at the other side one of the fight-promoters introduced the long king. Eagerly the crowd watched and waited for the action, but for almost two minutes nothing happened.

"Push 'em together!" a man called.

Taking up the long thin poles kept for that purpose, two of the promoters gently eased the snakes into the centre of the pit until they were only inches apart. Normally such an action would have been unnecessary, but even when up close the king showed no aggressive tendencies despite the fact that it ought to be hungry enough to want to make a meal of the first snake it saw.

"Make 'em come to taw!" suggested a spectator. "Damn-it, neither of 'em wants to fight."

As the promoter eased the king closer, the brightly coloured snake coiled, reared and struck, its fangs driving into the other's body just below the head. Fast though the king tore free and tried to throw its coils about the other, the gay-hued snake slipped away. Then the king began to thrash around wildly, knotting itself and beating its tail in frenzy as if fighting off some attack. Just what that attack might be, none of the crowd could imagine. Millbanks' snake had slithered to the far side of the pit and coiled up, ignoring the struggles of the king. At last the king stopped struggling and lay still.

Silence dropped on the crowd, their excited comments dying away. Not one of them could imagine what might have happened in the pit. Never had they seen a king snake laid low by a single bite; and from such a slender specimen of a critter too.

"Now's our chance!" Riegel hissed in Fanning's ear and caught the other roughly by the sleeve, turning him. "You lousy cheat, there's something crooked going on here!"

Every eye swung towards the two men and suspicious, profane discussions began to develop. None of the crowd knew Millbanks' entry to be a harlequin coral snake the captain picked up in Mexico, or that *Elaps Fulvius'* poison differed from that of the *Crotalids* over which the kings scored so many victories. While the pit-vipers—rattle-snakes, copperheads and water moccasins—used poison which attacked the blood of the victim, a coral snake's venom destroyed the nervous system; which accounted for the defeat of the king after only one bite. Not knowing the facts, the members of the crowd who had lost money on the result suspected that in some way they had been cheated.

"Let loose!" Fanning howled, following his part of the plan. Placing both his hands against Riegel's chest he began to push and yelled, "Get your cotton-picking hands offen me!"

Releasing Fanning's arm, Riegel went reeling away as if out of all control. He hurled straight for where Dusty, Belle and Millbanks stood at the edge of the pit. Just too late Dusty saw their danger and tried to thrust Belle to one side. Riegel changed course slightly, cannoned into the girl and sent her sprawling over the edge of the pit. Shouts rose and some fights broke out as the over-excited crowd saw Fanning's action. Cursing, yelling warnings, the promoters rushed to protect and prevent being opened the boxes containing poisonous snakes needed for other fights.

Belle fell backwards, winded by the impact, and landed on the soft sand of the pit. Riding instincts helped her to break her fall, but what she saw jolted all cohesive thought from her mind.

Out in the centre of the pit, the coral snake had become aware of the open nature of the surrounding area; a condition it would never have endured in its natural state. The vibrations of Belle's arrival in the pit caused the coral to go into a defensive coil. Then it located the girl's body and, not recognizing Belle for a human being, saw only the cover and shade it craved. Swiftly the coral snake began to glide towards the girl.

Hearing the scream which broke unchecked from Belle's lips, Dusty forgot his intention of taking apart with his bare hands the man who caused the trouble. Without a moment's hesitation or thought of the danger to himself, Dusty leapt into the pit. His feet missed the snake's tail by less than half an inch and he did not fancy chancing trying to hit a moving, slender mark like the snake with a shot taken after a fast draw. Which left him only one thing to do.

Down shot his right hand, a hand capable of drawing a gun with blinding speed—although his true potential in that line would not become fully perfected until in 1873 when the Colt factory produced its Model P, the gun which became the greatest fighting revolver ever made*—stabbed down and closed on the snake's tail. Dusty's original intention had been to jerk up the snake, crack it like a whip and snap its back in at least two places, immobilizing it quickly. However, something at the corner of his eye drew his attention to the side of the pit. What he saw caused him to change his plans for disposing of the snake.

*Told in THE PEACEMAKERS by J. T. Edson. Wagon Wheel Western W315.

Riegel stood on the edge of the pit, unseen by any of the crowd. Even Millbanks, busy explaining to objecting betters about his snake, failed to notice Riegel aiming a twin barrelled Remington Double Derringer down into the pit. If any of the arguing, excited crowd noticed the man, they must have thought him about to shoot the coral snake in an attempt to save the girl and Dusty.

Maybe Dusty would have thought the same had he not seen that the deadly little gun was aimed at Belle and not the snake. In that moment Dusty knew the incident was not accidental. The man deliberately pushed Belle into the pit and meant to kill her. Seeing his first plan fail, Riegel now meant to use his gun; either escaping in the confusion, or swearing that he tried to shoot the snake and how the girl moved into the line of fire as he squeezed the trigger.

With Dusty, to think had become nature to act. Even as his hand closed on the snake's tail, he had seen Riegel and formed his own conclusion. Whipping the snake up, Dusty flung it straight at Riegel's head. Even the most confirmed Union supporter, fanatically dedicated to destroying the South's top woman spy, would have flinched and forgotten his plans at the sight of that flying snake. Riegel served the Union for money and had no fanatical loyalty to support him. Desperately he threw up his gun-hand in an attempt to fend off the snake. He felt its sinewy length strike his arm, then coil around it. Like a flash, the enraged snake struck forward and up. Riegel screamed as he felt the burning sensation on the side of his neck. Horrified eyes turned towards him, staring at the gaily-coloured coral snake which swung by its jaws from his throat.

All quarrelling and fights became forgotten as the crowd saw Riegel spin around then crash to the ground. The snake fell away and started to wriggle. Jumping forward, Millbanks stamped down with his boot, its heel crushing the snake's head to a pulp.

"Get the man who pushed him!" Dusty yelled, springing to Belle's side.

However, before anybody could think straight enough to obey, Fanning had fled without a trace. Nor would they learn anything from Riegel. The coral snake had not used much poison to kill the king and its venom sacs contained more than enough to write a speedy *finis* to Riegel; especially when bitten in the neck and so close to the controlling mechanism of the nervous system, the brain.

Millbanks sprang forward to help Belle out of the pit and Dusty looked around him, seeing no sign of Riegel's companion.

"What the hell happened?" asked Millbanks.

"I'll tell you later," Dusty replied. "Now let's get the hell out of here."

## CHAPTER THIRTEEN

## Miss Boyd Meets An Informer

Lying fully dressed on her bed in the best room of the Plaza Dixie Hotel, Belle Boyd looked up at the roof and smiled wryly. It seemed ironic that she who had given so much and taken so many chances for the South should be regarded as *persona non grata* in a Confederate Army officers' mess. Of course she realized that if she had announced her true identity, the mess door would be flung open and a welcome accorded to her; but she could not let it be known that she was Belle Boyd.

So Belle found herself alone. The local garrison issued invitations for "General" Amesley and his staff to be guests at dinner and, rather than go into lengthy explanations or arouse suspicions, the three officers accepted. At which point a snag cropped up. While the local officers' ladies would have felt honoured to make the acquaintance of *the* Captain Dusty Fog of the Texas Light Cavalry, they strenuously and vocally objected to meeting a non-combatant general's *aime* on social grounds. Showing remarkable tact, the garrison commander avoided the issue by making the affair a strictly male function.

After some argument, Dusty and the other two left Belle in the hotel. Dusty warned her not to go out, remembering that one of the men who nearly caused her death at the snake-fight pit escaped and might want to try again. Smiling a little at the small Texan's concern for her welfare, Belle agreed to remain in the hotel and spend as much time as possible in the safety of her room.

After the incident at the snake-pit, things moved fast. First the local law was summoned and, sizing up the officer correctly, Dusty took him aside to tell him almost the full story. Being a stout Southron as well as a peace officer, the town marshal only needed to learn Belle's identity to make him willing to cover up the killing of Riegel as an accident. With the legal side cleared, Belle spoke to Millbanks and found him willing to take them to Matamoros. He could not sail until the following afternoon, but Belle suggested that the bulk of the luggage, including most of the money, went aboard immediately. Accepting the girl's judgment, the men made all necessary arrangements and transferred the baggage to the safety of the *Snow Queen*. Doing so left them free to accept the garrison officers' invitation, but doomed Belle to a lonely, boring night at the hotel.

She wore one of her specially designed skirts and a plain white blouse, not bothering to dress formally when going to dinner in the hotel. Relaxed in her room after the meal, she turned over the events of the day in her mind. Given time, she could have tried to trace the man who made the attempt on her life. As she would be sailing the following day, the best she could do was hand the matter to the local branch of the Confederate States Secret Service. They knew of the existence of the ring and might possibly be able to trace it through the dead man.

A knock on the door interrupted her thoughts on how

she would handle the investigation. Rising, she crossed the room to find the fat, pompous desk clerk outside.

"There is a person downstairs asking to see you, ma'am," he announced in a voice which showed that he did not approve of the "person" as being suitable to visit a guest at the hotel. "He sent up this note."

Taking the grubby envelope offered to her, Belle first noticed that its flap had been sealed down. Obviously the sender did not intend to have the message read by a snooping hotel employee during its delivery to Belle. Tearing open the flap, she extracted a sheet of equally grubby paper and looked down at the one line of writing upon it.

*"I have something to sell to you, Miss Belle Boyd."*

Slowly Belle's eyes lifted to the man's face, but she had such control over her emotions that he never noticed any change in her expression. "Who brought this for me, please?"

"A pedlar called Jacobs," the clerk replied. "He has a hat box with him."

"Then you can bring him up."

"Up *here?*" yelped the man.

"It's quite proper for a lady to interview a tradesman in privacy," she smiled. "He's probably bringing me a new hat I ordered."

After the man left, Belle closed the door, went to her bed and drew out the small bag which contained her overnight items. Reaching into the bag, she took out an object which she concealed under the bed's covers. Shortly after, the clerk ushered in a tall, thin, bearded and dirty-looking man of Hebraic appearance. Pausing for a moment as if waiting for an invitation to stay and act as chaperon, the clerk gave an indignant sniff when it did not come, turned and left the room. Belle's visitor swung on his heel and thrust the door into a closed position and faced the girl—to look into the barrel of the Dance she produced from beneath the bed covers.

"I don't know you, Mr. Jacobs," she stated.

"I'm only a poor Jewish pedlar, Miss Boyd," he replied, standing very still. "A famous lady like you wouldn't know the likes of me."

"Then you want something?"

"Only to make a few cents trading."

"What have you to trade?" Belle asked, looking down at the large hat box in Jacobs' hands."

"Something a bit more valuable than a hat."

"Put the box down and tell me more."

Setting the box on the floor, Jacobs looked up at the girl. "Is that business, telling what I know before we talk money."

"It's how I do business," Belle warned. "We'll start with you telling me how you know my name."

"Come now, Miss Boyd," Jacobs purred. "A business man never tells his sec—"

His words trailed away as he stared at Belle. Still keeping the gun in her right hand lined at the man, Belle reached towards her middle with her left. The skirt she wore had been designed with the needs of her profession in mind and a pull on the buckle freed the waist band, allowing the skirt to drop free to the floor. Underneath Belle did not wear petticoats and the removal of the skirt left her lower regions exposed; which proved to be quite an eye-bugging sight. Her drawers were considerably shorter than a young lady of good-breeding usually employed as buttock covering. Suspender straps made black slashes down the white thighs and connected with black silk stockings. The contrast of colours served to show Belle's magnificent legs to their best advantage. High-heeled, calf-length shoes graced her feet and added to the general sensuous effect.

While never having heard the word, Belle was aware of the psychological impact the removal of her skirt and appearance it left would have upon Jacobs. He stood with his mouth trailing open and eyes bugging out like organstops, feasting his licentious gaze upon her lower limbs.

"I learned *savate* in a New Orleans academy," she remarked. "It's very painful, as you will find out if I don't get my answers."

"Suppose I walk out?" he asked, his voice a trifle hoarse.

Without taking her Dance out of line, Belle threw up her left leg in a standing high kick that rose with sufficient power and height to rip off half his nose if it connected. Although Belle stood some distance away, Jacobs retreated hurriedly until his back struck the wall.

"Is there any need for all this foolishness?" he asked in what should have been a growl but came out as a whine. "I came here in all good faith to see you—"

"How did you learn my name?" Belle interrupted and delivered a horizontal stamping side kick which dented the brass knob on the bed post, still without taking her gun out of line. "Don't try to open the door; I'll shoot you and swear that you attacked me, if you try it."

Jacobs hurriedly jerked his hand away from the door handle. Not for a moment did he doubt that the girl meant every word she said. Anybody playing the dangerous game of spying could only be a success and stay alive by possessing a ruthless nature and no false sense of the value of human life.

"I was on the dock this morning when the *Rosebud* came in," he yelped. "Feller next to me pointed to you and said, 'That's Belle Boyd. I saw her in Atlanta.' Well, I told this feller to keep quiet as we didn't know who might be listening and he shut his mouth. Only I'd heard him. Seeing's how I'd something that the South needs, I thought you'd be the best market."

"You're *selling* information that could help the South?" she hissed.

"I'm only a poor man, Miss Boyd. Trade's become bad these days. A man has to make a living."

"What have you to sell?" she snapped.

"It's worth a hundred dollars," Jacobs answered. "In gold."

"Land-sakes!" Belle gasped. "Do you have the entire war plans of the Yankee Army?"

"No!" growled the man.

"I can't think of anything else that would be worth a whole hundred dollars in gold."

"How about a buried telegraph wire running from Morgan City to the mouth of Atchafalaya Bay, the other end being visited by men from the Yankee blockade ships every night to take word of ships leaving the dock?"

"You're either joking, or lying," Belle remarked, hiding the interest she felt. "Which is it?"

"Can I open the hat box?"

"Do it real slow and watch what you bring out. Make sure I can see what you are doing all the time."

Moving slowly, Jacobs raised the lid of the box and placed his hand inside. He used only the tips of his thumb and forefingers to bring an object into sight and toss it on to the bed.

"Go and lean forward with both hands against the wall and your feet spread well apart," Belle ordered, not touching or looking at the object.

"Don't you trust me?" Jacobs whined.

"In a word, no," the girl answered. "Go do what I said."

Not until Jacobs had assumed a posture which did not allow swift movement did Belle relax and study the object he tossed to her. Only by exercising all her will-power did she prevent an exclamation of surprise leaving her. The thing on the bed was a new model sending and receiving key which bore the markings of the U.S. Military Telegraph Department on it.

"Does this prove anything?" she sniffed. "You can stand up and turn around."

Obeying the order, Jacobs waved a hand towards the machine. "It proves there is a telegraph station around here."

"Or that you picked up the key from some soldier who collected it on the battlefield."

"When I see the money, I'll tell you where the station is."

Reaching into her vanity bag, Belle took out and flipped two double eagles to the man. He caught them and tested each with his teeth, but made no attempt to examine the dates.

"I said a hun—" he began.

"*If* we find the station you can collect the other sixty," Belle replied.

Jacobs thrust the money into his pocket and gave a shrug. "This's the last time I ever do anybody a good service."

"You'll make me weep in a minute," Belle answered. "Where is it?"

"Down back of the cat-house—that's a—"

"I know what it is; and where."

"Down back of the cat-house there's an old fisherman's cabin. Empty now, or was. The station's in there, keys hid under the floorboards."

"Sounds awful chancy to me," Belle said. "Anybody might go in there and find the station."

"Not many folks go down that way. The folks at the cat-house don't take to having prowlers around back. A lot of their sports wouldn't want it known they go down there."

"I suppose not," Belle smiled, then became serious again. "Suppose they, the Yankees, miss that key?"

"It's a spare, I left the box it was in. Maybe they won't notice for days."

"All right. Come around tomorrow and I'll give you the other sixty—if I find you've told the truth."

"Are you going there yourself?"

"Me? Certainly not. I'll send along a troop of soldiers. Get going—and if you tell anybody my name, I'll see you regret it."

"I'm an honest pedl—" Jacobs protested.

"I'm sure you are," Belle purred. "But watch what you peddle. A man could meet with a bad end, trading in some kind of goods."

A few years later Belle's warning may have come back to Jacobs as he was shot down by a member of a criminal gang that he had tried to sell to the Texas Rangers.*

After Jacobs left Belle's room, the girl closed and locked the door. Swiftly she turned his information over in her head. Knowing the manner in which professional informers could gather items of interest, she wondered how much of Jacobs' story might be true. She doubted if he learned her name in the manner he claimed, although it could just possibly be true; she had been a blonde while working against the Yankee spy-ring in Atlanta and still used the same wig. Then her eyes went to the telegraph key. It was a model only recently introduced, not one of the old *Beardslee Patent Magneto-Electric Field Telegraph* machines with which the Yankees went into the War and that failed to stand up to the rugged usage of active service. Of course the key could be a souvenir picked up on some battlefield, but it seemed to be in too good condition for that.

For a moment Belle thought of sending word to Dusty or the members of the local Secret Service field office and asking for assistance. Then a thought held her. Despite the fact that they had proved their worth many times over, Belle Boyd, Rose Greenhow and other female members of their organization still found a certain reluctance on the part of the Confederate States armed forces' top brass to recognize their use. Many of the senior officers clung to the belief that a woman's place was in the home and objected to Southern ladies being allowed to do such work as spying. If word got out that Belle had fallen for an ancient

*Told in THE COW THIEVES by J. T. Edson. Wagon Wheel Western W329.

informer's trick and wasted good money on a false alarm, further fuel would be added to the flames of objection which blazed whenever the subject of women spies rose in high places.

So Bell decided to make the preliminary investigation herself. Nothing dramatic, of course, like trying to take the station single-handed, but enough to ensure that she would not waste time or lose prestige by sending the men from the field office on a wild-goose chase.

The overnight bag held her dark blue shirt, riding breeches and gunbelt and it was work for a moment to change out of the clothes she wore to dinner. After strapping on the belt and holstering her Dance, she drew back the covers and, using the bag, her wig and items from the room, made what would pass for a sleeping shape in the bed. If anybody should happen to look into her room, she did not want an alarm raised through her absence. Leaving the hotel offered no difficulty, even if she could not use the stairs and front door for obvious reasons. In case of fire, each room had a coil of rope secured to the wall near its window. Belle raised the window sash, tossed out the rope and slid down it hand over hand to the street at the rear of the hotel. Being used only for tradesmen delivering to the businesses lining the main street, nobody walked the area into which Belle slid. She paused for a moment to get her bearings, then walked along the back street. By keeping to the shadows, she hoped to reach her destination without attracting any attention.

After leaving Belle's room, Jacobs hurried downstairs and passed through the hotel lobby. The desk clerk scowled, but said nothing, figuring that the pedlar must have made a sale as he did not carry the hat box. On the street outside the hotel, Jacobs threw a cautious look in either direction before walking hurriedly away. He went fast, with many a backwards glance. Making sure that he was not followed, Jacobs passed through the entertainment section of the town and reached the small, unobtrusive building which housed the Yankee spy-ring. Apparently he was known there, for the bouncer admitted him and led him to the office used by the madam.

Flora lounged on the couch when the door opened, but she came to her feet as she recognized her visitor.

"Well?" she said, as the door closed behind Jacobs.

"I saw her and did like you told me. She fell for it."

"And she agreed to come look the cabin over?"

"Sure she—"

"You're a liar!" Flora snapped out. "What did she really say?"

"Th—That she'd send soldiers."

"That's more like the Boyd I know," Flora purred. "Now get the hell out of here and keep going. My men'll be watching to make sure you don't go near anybody else to peddle your wares."

"I—I'm loyal to the North!" Jacobs wailed.

"Then the best I can wish is that you'd go over to the other side," Flora replied. "Get going."

At the door, Jacobs turned and looked back at Flora. "It looks like your idea didn't work."

"Yes," she agreed. "It looks that way."

However, after Jacobs left the room Flora gave a cold, calculating smile. While she expected Belle to tell the man that soldiers would make the investigation, Flora knew the Southern spy would only do this as a precaution, and was certain to look into the matter herself.

That was why Flora acted as she did. Why she sent the telegraph key and told of the message-passing station which had been set up at such hardship and effort. One of the spies exposed by Belle Boyd in Atlanta had been more than just a friend, he was Flora's brother and met his end standing back to a wall while facing a line of Confederate Army rifles. Since that time Flora had prayed for an opportunity to lay her hands on Belle Boyd. Now chance threw the rebel spy Flora's way and she did not intend to miss her opportunity—even if she had to use the most valuable secret her ring possessed as bait to draw Belle into her power.

Going to the room's second floor, Flora looked out and called, "Beth, May!"

Two tall, buxom girls, a brunette and a blonde, entered the room. Wearing cheaply garish frocks and jewellery, they gave an impression of hard flesh under the tawdry finery.

"She's going to be there?" asked May, the brunette.

"It's all arranged," Flora agreed.

"We'll teach her that no lousy madam's going to open another place up close to our house," Beth spat out.

While Flora reckoned her girls could be relied upon not to support either side in the War, she thought it might be better if the two selected to side her believed they dealt with a rival madam who planned to convert the old fisherman's cabin into a house which would steal some of their trade, rather than mention that the woman they were to attack was the South's most legendary Belle Boyd.

"Sure we will," Flora agreed, glancing at the girls' hands. "Take those rings off before we go."

Both girls opened their mouths to object, knowing the value of the heavy, embossed rings offered for offence and defence. However, Flora insisted. The girls thought that all they would do was work their victim over, leaving her a battered but wiser woman. Flora aimed to make sure that Belle Boyd never spied again. Knowing that the disappearance of so important a person would cause a stir, Flora aimed to take no chances. The town marshal was no fool and knew an indecent amount of things one did not expect of a small town lawman—he had been a captain on the New Orleans Police Department before the arrival of the Yankees; keen, conscientious, the kind who kept up with the latest developments in criminal investigation. Flora intended to dump her enemy's body in the bay where the alligators would dispose of it, but knew that something might go wrong. Faced with a badly battered body, the marshal knew enough to understand the significance of any ring-cuts on the face. He would know that somewhere were rings that bore traces of human skin and blood. While the rings might inflict more damage on Belle Boyd, Flora did not want them using if doing so helped the law to locate her.

With the rings removed, the girls followed their employer from the house and went to the cabin where they made their preparations for the arrival of their prey.

## CHAPTER FOURTEEN

## A Demonstration of La Savate

Approaching the fisherman's shack, Belle Boyd studied it with distaste. Set close to the edge of Atchafalaya Bay, the building did not exude a welcoming air. Small, one-roomed, dark and deserted, yet still in reasonable condition, was how the cabin appeared to the girl. All around her the mangrove swamp and canebrakes closed in, making the winding path along which she walked gloomy, eerie almost, when one listened to the mysterious noises of the swamp-land at night.

If she had seen a light, or anything to hint that the telegraph station's crew were present, Belle would have returned to town and gathered assistance. No coward, Belle also did not rank folly among her achievements. While she could handle a revolver with some skill, matching shots against a bunch of desperate Yankee spies would prove too much for her. She knew her capabilities and recognized her limitations. If forced to by circumstances, she would have tackled the gang, but given a chance or choice in the matter, she intended to fetch help to make more certain the capture and destruction of the Yankee's message-distribution organization. Finding the building in darkness, she decided to check and confirm Jacobs' information.

Drawing her Dance, she approached the front door of the building. She doubted if the Yankees maintained a guard on the cabin when not using it; to do so might invite unwanted curiosity. In all probability the telegraph key would only be connected when in actual use and might even not be present at other times. However, the wires could not be rolled up and hidden between messages. Finding them would be all the proof she needed.

Gently she gripped the door handle, twisting and shoving at it. The door opened silently, a significant point that Belle grasped. If the cabin had been unused for some time, its hinges ought to screech a protest when working. Trying to peer through the stygian blackness of the building's interior, Belle moved forward. Eyes and ears worked hard to pick up any hint of danger; but her nose made the first detection. The significance of the faint aroma of perfume did not, however, strike her quite quickly enough. Even as she realized that such a scent had no place in a Yankee spy-ring's telegraph station, a hand caught her shoulder, jerked hard and heaved her towards the darkness in the centre of the cabin.

Taken by surprise, Belle had no chance to resist. The hand gripped her and pulled hard; as she shot forward, Belle heard the door slam to. The light flooded the room from a lantern hanging in the centre. Belle saw a big brunette stood with hands still gripping the lantern's covers, but that one did not constitute the immediate danger. Unable to halt her forward rush, Belle advanced straight into the round-arm swing the waiting Flora launched at her. Woman-like, Flora used the flat of her hand instead of her knuckles. Even so, the force of the slap sent Belle spinning across the room and caused her to drop her gun. Pain knifed through her and her head spun from the blow. Only just in time did she manage to twist herself around so that she struck the wall shoulders first instead of colliding face-on.

"Get her!" Flora screeched.

Only one thing saved Belle. The two girls aiding Flora expected to be confronted by a rival cat-house madam dressed in the conventional manner. Unable to see more than a blurred shape in the doorway, Beth carried out her part in the plan to perfection by grabbing Belle and thrusting her forward. Nor did May show any less ability in lighting the lantern at just the right moment. In doing so, she illuminated not a cat-house madam in a dress, but a beautiful girl wearing men's clothing and carrying a gun. The shock of the unexpected sight held Beth and May off for just that vital second Belle needed to regain control of her slap-scattered wits.

One thing Belle knew immediately and without needing any heavy thought, she must fight if she hoped to escape with her life. Although her Dance lay in the centre of the room, leaping for it would be suicide while all three of her attackers remained on their feet.

After screaming her order, Flora hurled herself straight at Belle. Fury and hate over-rode caution and made the redhead act without thinking of the consequences. Or it may have been that she believed a high-born Southern lady like Belle Boyd would prove easy meat. If that had been Flora's thought, she would swiftly find disillusionment.

Moving clear of the wall, and seeing the other girls recover from their surprise, Belle prepared to handle Flora's hair-reaching rush with something a damned sight more effective than curl-yanking. Up rose Belle's right leg until its calf was parallel to the floor and the sole of her high-heeled shoe aimed at Flora. Straightening her left leg, Belle leaned backwards slightly and thrust forward the right in a stamping high kick. Full into Flora's sizeable bust crashed the foot. Sick agony tore into the Union supporter; her eyes bulged and her mouth opened in a hideous shriek of pain. She stumbled backwards, momentarily out of the fight.

From her assault on Flora, Belle brought down her leg, pivoted and lashed up the kind of high kick which so impressed Jacobs at the hotel. Only this time she stood close enough to land home. The toe of her left boot caught Beth's top lip, although it must be admitted that Belle aimed to smash it under the other's chin, crushing the flesh up and splitting it before continuing to squash the nose. Squealing in agony, blood gushing from lip and nose, blinded by tears, Beth spun around and reeled away.

Fingers dug into Belle's hair from behind as her third attacker came within reaching distance. May lay on a one-handed hold, her other fist driving into Belle's back just above the kidney region. Even the back kick which Belle launched automatically, catching Mary just over the right knee, failed to release the tearing grip on the Southern girl's hair. It did, however, serve to hold the big brunette at arms' length instead of closing in to continue her assault. Fiery pain burst into Belle's head and almost drove thoughts of effective defence from it. Luckily she retained sufficient control to know that she must free herself before the other two attackers recovered and came to lend their friend a hand.

Tilting backwards as if dragged off balance, Belle brought up both hands to clamp over the fingers which still dug into her hair and pressed them firmly against her skull. Using her left leg as a pivot, Belle twisted around while still retaining her hold on the trapped hand and halted when she faced towards the other girl. May squealed as the leverage on her hand bent her wrist at an unnatural angle. On being released, her automatic reaction was to stagger back.

Up drove Belle's left foot, aiming at May's lower body. However, May had been in brawls before and, hurt or not, knew a thing or two. Her hands shot forward to catch Belle's kicking ankle.

"Come on, you pa—!" May began, feeling that her

companions left too much for her to handle alone.

The words were chopped off, for Belle knew more than a few tricks and was prepared against the possibility of someone trapping her in that manner during a kick. Twisting her body, she brought her free leg up from the floor, turning so it passed over the trapped limb. Drawing the left leg back, Belle stabbed it out in a stamp to the centre of May's face. Again May felt the sickening impact of the kick and it cut off her demand for assistance. She lost her hold and stumbled away, hand clawing to her bleeding nose.

A hand caught Belle by the shoulder as she landed. Another came around, drove into her stomach and as she doubled over a knee caught her in the face. Belle crashed into the wall, half-blinded by tears of pain. Digging fingers into Belle's hair, Flora heaved and threw the girl across the room. Only Belle's superb co-ordination kept her on her feet. Again she managed to turn and hit the wall with her back, bouncing off it in the direction of Beth as the blonde rushed forward. Belle reacted almost without thought, yet she brought off the ideal answer to Beth's rush. Bounding into the air, Belle drew up her legs and thrust them forward with all her strength. Too late Beth saw her danger. Her own forward impetus added force to the kick as Belle's boots drove full into her bust. Screaming in mortal agony, Beth shot backwards, twisted around and crashed brutally into the wall.

Rebounding from the leaping high kick, Belle landed on her feet and found fresh trouble. Leaping forward, Flora smashed a blow which caught Belle at the side of the face. Behind the red-head, May came forward again. Desperately Belle drove out a roundhouse right which exploded on the side of Flora's jaw and sent her staggering to one side. May skidded to a hurried halt on seeing that she must again face alone the devastating fighting techniques of the other girl. Deciding to make use of her superior reach. May flung a punch at the black-haired girl's head. Throw-

ing up her right fist, Belle caught the outer side of May's
striking arm, deflected the blow and turned the brunette's
body from her. A swift side-step put Belle in position to
deliver a stamping kick to the back of May's left knee.
Even as the bigger girl lost her balance, Belle's left foot
reached the floor and her right swung up to crash hard at
the base of the brunette's skull. Already off balance, the
kick flung May forward and, dazed and helpless, she
smashed headlong into the wall. From there she collapsed
in a limp heap upon the floor.

Before Belle could fully recover from handling May,
she found fresh trouble. Flora flung herself forward, coming in at Belle's side. Two arms locked around Belle's
waist and the impact knocked her sprawling to the floor with
Flora clinging to her. On landing, Belle forgot all her
knowledge of *savate* and her fingers dug into the mass of
red hair. An instant later she felt as if the top of her head
had burst into flames, for Flora retaliated in the same manner.

With both of Flora's girls out of action, the fight became equal. Over and over thrashed and turned the struggling gasping, squealing girls, first one then the other
gaining the upper position and holding it until thrown over
by the one on the bottom. In the earlier stages of the fight
Belle's clothing gave her a greater freedom of movement
than that afforded by the dresses of her attackers. Now the
advantage meant little in the wild, close-up tangle the fight
had become. Tearing hair, slashing wild slaps and blows,
flailing with their legs, fingers digging and twisting into
flesh, Belle and Flora churned about the room in a wild
female fracas where skill had no place.

Slowly the Southern girl's superior physical condition
began to show its effect. Flora did not lead a life conducive
to perfect health and began to tire under the continued ex-
ertion. Slowly, but just as surely as when the king snake
crushed out the diamondback's life at the snake-pit, Belle
began to gain the upper hand. Blood ran from her nostrils;

the shoulder and one sleeve of her shirt had been ripped away, but she ignored both as she fought for mastery over the half-naked, just as badly marked red-head.

A surging heave rolled Flora from the upper position. She landed on her back, too exhausted to make more than a token resistance as Belle threw a leg across her body and sat on her. Blind instinct sent Belle's fingers to the other's throat, for at that moment the Southern girl became the most primeval and deadly of all creatures, a furiously angry, hurt woman. All her upbringing and refinement was forgotten as her fingers tightened upon Flora's throat. Fear gave Flora strength. She arched her back in an attempt to throw Belle from her, but failed. Croaking, unable to breathe, her hands beat at the other girl's face, tried to claw at her shoulders, then went down, gripping the top of Belle's exposed underwear in an attempt to get at the flesh below.

At that moment sanity began to creep into Belle's mind again, or it may have been that some primeval instinct gave warning of her danger. Whatever the reason, Belle twisted her head around to see what the other two women were doing. May lay where she had fallen, but Beth dragged herself across the floor in Belle's direction. One hand supported and tried to give relief to the throbbing agony in the ultrasensitive area which caught the impact of Belle's leaping high kick; but the other held a four-inch bladed push-knife such as gamblers and women of Beth's profession often carried concealed about their persons. While Beth had obeyed orders and discarded her rings, she retained the knife in its garter sheath. Seeing a chance to get at the woman who inflicted such punishment and suffering upon her, Beth drew the knife and started to crawl across the floor.

As if sensing what her companion planned, Flora clung even tighter to Belle's clothing. Struggling savagely, Belle tried to either rip the cloth or drag herself out of Flora's grasp, for she knew she must escape the hold—or die.

Even as Beth gathered her pain-wracked body for a dive which would carry her on to Belle and drive home the knife, the Southern girl smashed a fist with all her strength into Flora's right breast. Shocking agony ripped through Flora, numbing her body and causing her hands to release their hold. Feeling herself free of the clutching fingers, Belle rolled from Flora. She did not move a moment too soon. Down hurled Beth, her pain-drugged brain failing to react to the changed situation. Instead of realizing that her enemy had gone, Beth carried through the plan formulated as she crawled across the floor—only she landed on Flora, not Belle. Down drove the push-knife, its point sinking just under the redhead's left breast and Beth's weight sent the blade in hilt-deep.

Landing on her back, Belle coiled up her legs and, as Beth reared up from the jerking, twitching body of the red-head, drove out both feet. The shoes smashed with sickening force into the side of Beth's head. Giving a low moan, she pitched off Flora and crashed to the floor.

For almost a minute Belle stayed on her back. Across the room, May moaned and tried to rise. The sight gave Belle an incentive to move. Dragging her aching body erect, she stood swaying and looking around at a room which seemed to roll and pitch like the deck of a ship. Seeing her gun lying on the floor, she staggered forward and picked it up.

The cabin's door burst open and Fanning entered. For a moment he stood staring in amazement at the sight which met his eyes. He did not recognize Belle as the woman he tried to kill at the snake-pit, but she identified him.

"What the hell?" he demanded, reaching towards his sagging jacket pocket.

Sick with exhaustion and pain though she might be, Belle could still react to such a threat. Up came the Dance she held, almost of its own volition it seemed—in later years Belle could never remember lifting the gun or pressing the trigger—and roared. In the confines of the cabin, the crack of the light gun sounded as loud as the boom of a Dragoon Colt. Through the pain-mists and powder smoke Belle saw the man jerk, stagger, hit the wall and slide down. Without waiting to see how badly hurt he might be, Belle ran staggering from the room and along the dark trail towards Morgan City.

Reaction to the events of the evening began to set in as Belle made her way towards the town. Her body seemed to give out a continuous throbbing ache, her head whirled with dizziness and nausea threatened to engulf her at any moment. Gun in hand she stumbled long the path, darting frantic glances about her.

Suddenly a man's shape appeared on the track ahead of Belle. She had just turned a corner which hid the shack from view and before she could halt saw the dark bulk blocking her way. Even as she tried to raise her gun, the man sprang forward and struck at her wrist. Feeling his fingers close around her arm, Belle acted almost instinctively. Up drove her knee, catching the man in a place guaranteed to make him release his hold. The man gave a strangled gasp of pain for, although Belle might be on the verge of collapse, the impact packed enough power to drive agony through him. Feeling the hand leave her wrist, she thrust the man aside, but three more shapes swarmed around her and other fingers closed on her.

"It's a gal!" announced a disbelieving voice.

Blending down, one of the others raised Belle's Dance, held its muzzle to his nose and sniffed at it. "Hold down the talk!" he snapped in an authoritative tone. "This's been fired. Then it was a shot we heard from down there."

Relief flooded through Belle as she recognized the voice of Morgan City's efficient town marshal—who also ran the local field office of the Confederate States Secret Service: a detail he had not confided to Dusty.

"Shout—Southrons hear your country call you," Belle gasped.

"What the—!" began the marshal on hearing the familiar password. "Show a light here, but keep it down."

"N—No light!" Belle objected. "Down at the fisherman's cabin—"

"Get down there, two of you," the marshal ordered. "Keep alert at it. How'd you feel, Tom?"

"—terrible," came the profane reply from Belle's assailant. "That danged gal near on ruined me. Who is she?"

"B—Belle—Boyd—" gasped Belle, then collapsed.

"After covering up for you and asking no questions down at the snake-pit," the marshal said grimly, "I figure we rated some co-operation from you."

Seated in the marshal's office, feeling stiff, sore and more than a little sorry for herself, although having received medical attention for her numerous bruises and minor abrasions, Belle nodded gravely.

"I didn't aim to go over your head, or try to show my superiority over you. But the information I *bought* might have been false and I didn't want anybody to know about that if it should be. And I'd no intention of moving in it there'd been a light showing or any sign of life."

"How'd you get mixed in this game anyhow?" the marshal inquired. "We've known about that outfit for some time, but couldn't get any proof. I began to get suspicious when I heard that soldiers and seamen were being filled with free liquor down there. That's not the cat-house way, unless somebody wanted the men drunk and talking. Anyhow, I sent a cousin of mine in, he's on furlough down here. He went dressed as a seaman and found that after he'd been liquored up, Flora started asking him questions about when his ship would be sailing and what she'd carry. So I figured it was time we moved in and took a look around."

"Did you find the telegraph station?"

"Sure. That feller you shot, Fanning, he talked up a storm and showed us all we wanted. We raided the cat-house—don't know what the mayor'll have to say about it thought."

"Why should he have anything to say?" Belle asked.

"He was with one of the girls when we arrived—and him supposed to be at a meeting of the municipal council."

"If he's married, he won't say a word," Belle stated, and her guess proved to be correct. "Did you destroy the station?"

"Nope. I aimed to, but when I found Flora's code books, I figured that it might be useful to be able to let the Yankees know what we want them to know."

"It will be at that," Belle agreed. "Can you get word out that there won't be any ships leaving, but that one is expected from the north tomorrow night?"

"Sure we can. The Yankees land to take any messages at midnight every night. I'll tend to it for you."

"And how about that pedlar, Jacobs?" the girl went on. "He was the one who told me about the telegraph station."

"If I know old Jake Jacobs, he'll be long gone by now," the marshal replied. "Reckon that Flora sent him with the information for you?"

"She may have done. Did the two girls tell you anything yet?"

"Nope. May's in no shape to talk and all Beth knows is that you were supposed to be some cat-house madam who intended to open a place down there."

"They weren't in the spy ring?"

"I doubt it. The bouncer, Flora and a couple more were the only ones involved in the ring. I'll pick up the odd ends tonight. Got the boys started on it right now. We've bust the Yankee spy-ring. Say, one way and another, the Yankees have been giving you a bad time."

"I must have riled them for some reason," Belle smiled. "And now I'd best be getting back to the hotel. Lord knows what Dusty and the others will say when they see my face in the morning."

A grin creased the marshal's features as he studied Belle's blackened right eye, scratched cheek, swollen lip and nose. "You might try telling them you walked into a door and it fought back."

## CHAPTER FIFTEEN

## A Difference of Table Manners

Although Belle's appearance attracted some comment among her friends, all found themselves too busy preparing for their departure the next day to go too deeply into the matter.

From that smooth manner in which the trip went, it seemed that the gods of war had relented and decided to smooth the path for their small band of devotees.

Slipping from her berth, the *Snow Queen* ran down the Atchafalaya Bay under sail power on the evening tide. The false message had done its work and the Yankee blockade gun-boats lay to the north awaiting the arrival of the non-existent ship. By running the *Snow Queen* through a channel skirting the mangrove swamps which lined the shore, Millbanks avoided detection and at dawn lay well beyond the enemy's range of vision. Once clear, the crew profanely informed the Texans, no damned Yankee scow ever built could lay alongside the ole *Queen* in a stern chase.

In good weather and bad, the *Snow Queen* ran down to

the southwest at a steady thirteen knots. Showing masterly skill, Millbanks avoided the Yankee ships blockading Galveston, skimmed along the shore of Matagorda Island, beat out to sea to avoid the enemy off Corpus Christi and passed along the fringes of the shoals surrounding the elongated Padre Island. On approaching the mouth of the Rio Grande, the ship again put out to sea and slipped by in the night, unseen by a Yankee ironclad which lay a good three miles out from the entrance to the border river.

Thinking back on the trip, Duty decided that Millbanks must have augmented his winter earnings by doing in-shore trading—a polite name for smuggling—as he knew all the tricks of avoiding detection by an enemy and every channel of deep waters along which a vessel could slip close to the shore. The thought gained support on seeing the way the Mexican population of a small fishing village some twenty miles south of Matamoros greeted the *Snow Queen*'s arrival.

Using keg pontoons, Millbanks' men ferried ashore the carriage and horses brought aboard in Morgan City. Then the captain supplied a guide; a villainious-looking Mexican whom none of the Texas would have cared to trust without such good references. Certainly they had no cause to complain about his services. After arranging for Millbanks to wait in the area for a week or so as to be able to carry the arms, Dusty's party took to a form of transport they understood. Their guide led them along narrow, winding tracks through the swamp-lands of the coast and across the range to the Los Indios trail. There he left them and, following their original plan, the party entered Matamoros as if they had crossed the Rio Grande up Mercedes way and come along the river trail.

Despite Ole Devil's predictions, the party had little trouble with the bad elements of Matamoros society. On their arrival Amesley presented his credentials to the garrison commander, a bulky French general very much of *du peuple* and, like many of his kind, determined to appear gentile. One meeting told Amesley all he needed to know of the French general's nature and at the earliest opportunity he broached the subject of the exchange of deserters. Amesley's judgment paid off. While the garrison commander wanted to lay his hands on French deserters, using their fate as a deterrent to other would-be absconders, he refused to accept responsibility for such an important matter. Nor would he flatly refuse the offer. As Amesley expected, the French general insisted that the Texans stay on in Matamoros as his guests until he could send a report to Mexico City and receive instructions from higher authority.

Given a good excuse to stay in Matamoros, Amesley settled down to enjoy himself. There were parties to attend, dinner invitations to accept. For three days the Texans and Belle relaxed, although each day saw Dusty and the girl at the dockside watching for the first sign of Smee's boat.

To avoid attracting too much attention, Dusty and Red had discarded their gunbelts and now wore the regulation type of equipment, one revolver butt forward in a closed-topped holster at the right side, and a sabre in the slings at the left. Neither their skirtless tunics nor the fact that Dusty's Colt bore a white bone handle were out of character, as the Confederate Army allowed its officers considerable freedom in choice of arms and dress. Being introduced as Captain Edward Marsden, and the fact that he did not look how people imagined a man like Dusty Fog would be, prevented anyone suspecting his true identity. However, the open-topped holsters could have aroused suspicion, so Dusty left them off. He did not expect to need his weapons. True, there were some Yankee personnel in Matamoros, but they ignored the Southrons as became enemies meeting on neutral ground.

General Plessy laid great stress on his determination not to have trouble between Southrons and Yankees in his town. At the first meeting, he demanded that Amesley explain the rules of neutrality to the junior officers and warned that any trouble would result in all concerned, on both sides, being placed under arrest until the end of hostilities. With that in mind, Dusty and Red walked warily in the presence of such Yankees as they met and avoided conflict.

On the fourth afternoon a new ship had arrived and lay in the stream. Named the *Lancastrian,* she was an ugly vessel. A three-masted ship converted to steam propulsion, she retained her raised poop deck and standing rigging. The construction of the *Lancastrian* interested Dusty and Belle far less than the flag she wore.

"That's Smee's ship, Dusty," Belle said.

"She's not coming right in," he replied.

"I never thought she would. We'll go out by rowing-boat and visit with her captain."

"*We* will," Dusty agreed. "But not the money until after I'm satisfied that the arms are worth it."

"You've got a suspicious mind, Captain Fog," smiled the girl.

"Why sure," Dusty grinned back. "But I only got it *after* I tied in with you."

An hour later, after returning to the hotel which housed them and making all the necessary arrangements, Belle and Dusty sat in a shore-boat handled by a burly Mexican and skimmed towards the *Lancastrian.* The ship now rocked gently at anchor and a gangway hung down the side. With considerable skill, the Mexican boatman laid alongside the gangway and Dusty took out money to pay him.

Belle climbed the gangway ahead of Dusty and stepped on to the deck, halting to look around her. Some half a dozen or so seamen dressed in the usual fashion stood about, eyeing her with interest, but she ignored the glances, directing her attention to the two men who approached. Captain Smee looked much the same as on their previous meeting; tall, gaunt, miserable of feature. However, she could not recall having seen the tall, powerful man who followed on his heels. Clearly this one was a ship's officer, for he wore the same style peaked hat as

Smee, a frock coat and trousers tucked into seaboots.

"Good afternoon, Captain Smee," Belle greeted, sensing that the man did not recognize her.

Then recognition came to Smee's face. "It's Miss Tracey, isn't it?" he said. "But you had—"

"We ladies do change the colour of our hair occasionally," Belle smiled. "May I present Captain Edward Marsden of the Confederate States army. Captain Marsden, this is Captain Smee, of whom I have told you, and—"

"My—mate," Smee introduced, reading the question in Belle's unfinished sentence and inquiring glance at the other office. "Mr. Stone."

Apparently Stone belonged to the strong, silent class, for he acknowledged the introduction with nothing more than a grunt and did not offer his hand. Ignoring the other's silence, Dusty looked around him and then turned to Smee.

"You don't have many men about, Captain."

"They're all—" Smee hesitated and threw a quick glance at Stone, then went on. "They're all ashore except for an anchor watch. I didn't want too many knowing about the arms."

That figured; Smee could find himself in serious trouble if it became known that he sold arms to the Confederate States while in a neutral port.

"Speaking of the arms," Belle put in. "May we see them?"

"They're in the forward hold," Smee answered. "Do you have the money?"

"It's on shore, and will stay there until I'm satisfied with the consignment, Captain," Dusty stated.

"Come this way then," Smee growled.

With Stone following on his heels, Smee led Belle and Dusty to the hatch which gave access to the forward hold. Climbing down, he turned the wick of a lantern hanging from a beam and illuminated the cargo. He waved a hand towards a long row of variously shaped boxes.

"There they are. The same weapons Miss Tracey saw in England."

"My apologies, sir," Dusty answered. "But I've my duty to do; and my orders are to check the arms before accepting them. You don't object?"

After throwing a quick glance in Stone's direction, Smee gave a shrug. "Why should I object. There's a crow-bar, open any box you want."

Picking up the bar Smee indicated, Dusty walked along the row of boxes. He noticed that a couple had been opened recently and gave them his first attention. Forcing up the lid, he lifted out one of the rifles. Although smoth-ered in grease, as one might expect, the weapon proved to be in excellent condition, and after a thorough cleaning would be ready for use. After selecting from three other rifle boxes, Dusty sampled among the boxes of ammuni-tion, again finding everything to be satisfactory.

"They'll do," he said, returning to the others. "When we get outside I'll signal to my men to fetch the money along."

"I explained to Captain Smee and Mr. Stone that we didn't consider it safe to have that much money standing on the dock for any length of time, Edward," Belle re-marked "The captain has invited us to take a meal with him while we're waiting. If it's all right with you, I've accepted."

"You're handling the play, Miss Tracey," Dusty agreed.

On the deck again, Dusty removed his campaign hat and waved it twice in an anti-clockwise direction over his head. Standing on the dock, Red saw his cousin's signal and sig-nified to that effect by repeating it. Turning, the young lieutenant swung astride his waiting horse and rode back towards the better part of town.

With the formalities handled, Smee led his guests to a door set in the poop deck. Beyond it lay his quarters, two fair-sized cabins which gave him far greater space and comfort than that allocated to his officers or men. In the first cabin a table lay set ready and Smee waved his guests into their seats. The taciturn Stone followed the party in and drew up a chair without saying a word.

Dusty looked around the cabin, glancing at a couple of good pictures on the walls, then towards an open case holding a pair of fine *epee de combat*. While not mentioning the swords, he wondered about them. Smee did not strike Dusty as being the kind of man who would own such weapons.

Following Dusty's gaze, Smee seemed to think that an explanation was needed. "I picked them up cheap," he remarked, nodding to the case. "There's always a good sale for a fine sword in Mexico."

At that moment the door opened and a steward entered. Yet he was a most unusual type of man to be handling such a sedentary occupation, being six feet tall, burly and weather-beaten. Carrying a large tray, he approached the table and began to serve out the soup course.

Conversation did not prove to be a success during the meal. Although Belle tried to draw Stone into speech, he restricted his answer to non-committal grunts or terse comments of "Yes" or "no." Nor did Smee improve matters, for he appeared to have little small talk. In fact he acted as nervous as a hound-scared cat, throwing many worried glances towards the cabin's main door.

While watching Smee, Dusty happened to glance in Stone's direction and noticed that the man held his knife in the left hand. So did Belle and Dusty if it came to that—but Smee used his right for the same purpose. Nothing Dusty had seen about Stone, apart from the mate's scarcity of conversation, hinted at a lack of knowledge of etiquette. Yet he sat holding his knife in the wrong hand—for a European.

A tingling sensation ran down Dusty's spine. At the same moment the steward leaned over to pass a plate to Smee and his white jacket trailed open. Underneath, strapped to his belt, hung a long-bladed sheath knife. Or was it just a sheath knife? A second look showed that the blade was curved and its handle had the shape of an old-time pistol's butt. Such a weapon had significant overtones to a man who studied weapons as Dusty had.

Casting a glance at Belle, Dusty tried to read from her face if she felt as concerned and uneasy as he did. Not by as much as a flicker of an eyelid could he decide and so sat back to await developments.

"Shore-boat coming off," announced a seaman, poking his head around the door after knocking.

The door closed again and the steward moved around the table, approaching it from behind Dusty's back and reaching out big hands towards the small Texan. Suddenly, and without giving any indication of his intentions, Dusty caught up the plate from before him and hurled it over his shoulder full into the steward's face. Taken by surprise, the man gave a startled yell as the plate shattered on striking him. He went back a couple of steps and before he caught his balance had Dusty's thrown-over chair wrapped around his legs.

In almost the same move that he hurled back the plate and thrust his chair from under him, Dusty's hands caught the edge of the table. With a heave, he tipped the table over into Stone's lap. The mate, starting to rise and reaching towards his waistband, let out a yell as plates, cups and other contents of the table cascaded into his lap. Pure instinct caused him to rise and back off hurriedly. His legs became entangled with his chair and it tipped over, bringing him crashing to the floor.

Smee began to rise, his face working and mouth opening to say, or shout, something. Under the circumstances Dusty did not dare waste time learning which. Coming erect as he hurled over the table, the small Texan pivoted and delivered a karate forward stamping kick which caught Smee in the centre of his chest, chopped off his speech unsaid and pitched him and his chair over.

"Get the hell out of here, Belle!" Dusty barked. "It's a trap."

Even as Dusty made his first move, Belle had been thrusting back her chair. Stone's continued silence had first aroused her suspicions, taken with the fact that she had not seen the man and been introduced to an entirely different first mate while in England. Nor had his breach of European table manners gone unnoticed by the girl. Belle had also seen the steward's knife, recognizing it for what it was. Everything added up to a highly disturbing fact. Somehow or other, she and Dusty had walked into trouble. Stone's silence meant that if he spoke, his accent would give him away as not being British. One did not need to be a mental genius to figure things out after reaching *that* conclusion.

Rising, Belle darted to the door of the cabin and pulled it open. The big seaman who brought word of the shore-boat's arrival stood outside. Seeing the girl, he sprang forward, hands lifting towards her. Belle rocked back a pace and slammed the door with all her strength; its sturdy timbers struck the man and staggered him back. Before he could recover and rush forward once more, Belle had slid home the bolts and spun around.

"Go through the night cabin and up on to the poop deck!" she shouted.

No seaman, Dusty did not know what the hell the girl meant by poop-deck; but he could only see one way out of the cabin now the main entrance was barred. Giving forth a string of good Yankee curses, the steward whipped out the naval dirk which had so interested Dusty—at that time the curved bladed variety still remained the more usual type issued to members of both U.S. and Confederate Navies and the pistol-grip handle was much favoured by Yankee seamen.

Steel rasped as the Haiman Bros. sabre slid from its sheath. Dusty cut across as the steward tried to block his way to the night cabin's door. A cry of pain burst from the man's lips as the blade of Dusty's sabre slashed into his right forearm. The knife clattered from a hand the steward would never use again and he reeled blindly aside, clutching at his wound as he went to his knees.

Belle made the door of the night cabin in one bound, jerking it open and running across to the companionway which led to the poop-deck entrance. Throwing a glance at Stone as the man rose and leapt towards the cased *epee de combat*, Dusty decided to put off a fight until after he warned his friends of their danger. Darting through the night cabin's door, he slammed it to and sprang across to the companionway, passing Belle without formality. One shove threw open the hatch cover and Dusty swung out on to the raised poop-deck. Already two of the seamen made their way towards the deck, cutlasses which had been kept hidden, but ready for use, gripped in their hands.

"Red!" Dusty roared, leaping to meet the men as they swarmed up the companionway. "It's a trap. Yeeah, Texas Light!"

In the shore-boat, which held all their property ready for a hurried departure on going aboard the *Lancastrian,* Red and the others heard Dusty's yell mingle with startled, pure Yankee curses from the watching seaman at the head of the gangway. Even as the significance of the seamen's speech struck Red, he saw them produce cutlasses.

"Yeeah!" he yelled in answer to Dusty's war shout. "Cold steel, Billy Jack. Watch the boatman, Major, Dick. Let's go Up and at 'em, Texas Light!"

Remembering the warnings given by the French about breaches of neutrality, Red thought fast and gave a necessary order. While a sword fight might pass unnoticed from the shore, one could be certain that the sound of shooting would attract attention. Apparently the Yankees appreciated that fact as well as did the Texans, for they met Red and Billy Jack's rush with cold steel instead of lead.

Belle drew herself on to the poop-deck as Dusty met the first rush from below and looked to see how she might best help out. A sound from below took her attention and she looked back in the direction from which she fled. *Epee* in hand, Stone burst from the day cabin and rushed up the companionway. While he saw Belle, he made the mistake of dismissing her as a factor. Going on his knowledge of Southern girls, gained in the days before the War, Stone expected Belle to do no more than scream a warning to the Texan who would most likely have plenty on his hands without that distraction.

Resting his sword hand on the edge of the hatch, Stone forced himself upwards. Like a flash, Belle raised her right leg and stamped it down hard. The high heel of her boot spiked into the back of Stone's hand, bringing a startled yelp and causing him to release his hold of the *epee*. Even as the sword clattered to the deck, Belle brought off a stamping kick to Stone's face and tumbled him back down the companionway. A glance across the deck warned her that she must help Dusty—and quickly before it was too late.

At first, Dusty held the two men from gaining a foothold on the poop-deck. Then he saw a third sailor in the act of swinging up from the main deck so as to climb the rail and attack from the flank. A swift bound to the rear carried Dusty into position, but he knew there would not be time to turn and use his sabre. Instead his left arm lashed around the back of his fist driving full into the climbing man's face and pitching him off his perch. While he had removed one danger, Dusty saw that the other two seamen had reached the deck and came rushing at him, one slightly ahead of the other.

Around and out lashed the leading man's cutlass. Dusty shot back his left leg and went into a near-perfect turning *passata sotto*. As the cutlass hissed over his head, Dusty thrust upward. The point of his sabre bit in under his attacker's breast bone and drove up to split his heart.

Unable to reach Dusty with his blade, due to his companion·blocking his way, the second man launched out a kick. The tip of his heavy seaboot smashed into Dusty's right shoulder and flung the young Texan over. Dusty's arm went numb and the sabre fell from his hand as he went rolling to the edge of the deck. At which point Belle took a very effective hand. A jerk at her waistband freed the skirt and she bounded clear to rush across the deck. For a vital instant the shock of her actions froze the seaman into immobility. While Belle had taken the precaution of wearing her riding breeches under the skirt, she still presented an eye-catching picture—more so to a man who had been at sea and away from female company for several months.

Sheer instinct made him beat at the flickering blade of Belle's *epee* and he realized that the girl meant her attack. Already two more men, one with his nose running blood, were climbing to the poop-deck and Belle knew she needed help.

"Red!" she shrieked, lunging and driving her *epee* into the first man's forearm. "Get up here quickly!"

While willing to obey, Red found carrying out the request difficult. He and Billy Jack might be better hands with a sword than the two men blocking their path, but fighting upwards put them at a disadvantage. It was all the two Texans could do to hold off the slashes launched at them and neither found chance to make an offensive. Watching from the shore-boat, Amesley thrust himself to his feet and mounted the ladder. Behind him, Dusty's striker remained watching the Mexican boatman and protecting the party's baggage. Advancing until he stood behind the two Texans, Amesley drew his *epee*. For a moment he waited, then saw his chance. Out flickered the blade, passing between Red and Billy Jack to sink into the thigh of one of their attackers. Jumping forward, Red smashed the hilt of his sabre against the side of the wounded man's head before he recovered from the shock of the sudden attack. The seaman hit the side of the gangway and plunged into the water. A moment later his companion went reeling back from a cut to the body launched by the gangling sergeant-major.

"Get to Dusty quick!" Amesley ordered.

Springing to the head of the gangway, Red and Billy Jack raced towards the stern and hoped they might arrive in time. Bursting from the entrance where he had been guarding the *Lancastrian's* crew, a seaman charged along the deck. Amesley halted and met the attack. While handicapped by his injured leg, he still retained the marvellous control of his sword which made him famous as a *maitre d'armes*. Clumsy slashing had never been a match for the skilled use of a point; and so it proved. Two quick parries, then a lunge and Amesley's *epee* tore into the sailor's body, dropping him bleeding to the deck.

On the poop Belle displayed her skill with a sword by holding back the attackers who tried to get by her. Fighting desperately, she gave Dusty time to rise. With his right arm still numb and useless, Dusty bent and caught up the sabre in his left hand. He came alongside Belle, caught a slash launched at him, deflected it and laid open its deliverer's belly by a quick *riposte*. Then he saw Stone appear once more at the hatch top. Before he could disengage from the seaman, Dusty watched Stone make the deck. Turning, the small Texan left Belle to handle the seaman and sprang to meet the advancing Stone.

Never had the ambidextrous ability Dusty developed as a boy—a kind of defence to draw people's attention from his lack of height—been of such use. With his right arm too numb and sore to be of use, he could still handle the sabre almost as well with his left. In fact the left-hand style of fighting, which Dusty adopted completely, gave Stone, used to handling opponents who fought from the right, some trouble. Taken with the fact that Stone had become accustomed to wielding a naval sword designed, like the sabre, for cut-and-slash tactics, Dusty's left-hand style kept him alive. Even so he knew it would be a close thing in his present condition. The two men came up close, sword hilts locking together. At one side Belle gave a quick glance at the men as they strained against each other and she knew the fight must be concluded speedily before somebody on shore noticed it and informed the authorities.

"Dusty!" she called, parrying her man's slashing attack which came too fast for her to get home a thrust in reply. "Re—member—family—motto—"

Up went her left hand, tearing off her hat and wig and flinging them into the seaman's face. Blinded and amazed at seeing the girl apparently tear off all her hair in one pull, the man staggered back. Like a flash Belle lunged and the *epee* took the man in the forearm causing him to drop his cutlass. He reeled back, struck the edge of the rail and fell to the deck.

Dusty's right foot rose and stamped down hard on to Stone's instep in a manner taught to him by Tommy Okasi. Pain knifed into Stone, causing him to yell and relax the pressure he put against Dusty's sabre. With a heave, Dusty thrust the man from him and Belle, turning from spitting the seaman, thrust her *epee* home. Steel bit through flesh, gliding between the ribs and into Stone's body. He stiffened, the weapon clattering from his hand as his knees buckled under him and he crumpled to the floor.

"Thanks, Belle!" Dusty said and sprang to the side of the deck.

Down below a battle raged between Red, Billy Jack and the remaining three Yankee sailors. Even as Dusty looked, Billy Jack received a slash across his shoulder, but Red ran one man through. Dusty's arm whipped back and he hurled his sabre downwards like a man throws a dart. Swinging up his cutlass to deliver a *coup-de-grace* to Billy Jack, the man who wounded the sergeant-major arched his back and fell, Dusty's thrown sabre sunk into his spine.

Seeing what had happened and that the small Texan left himself weaponless, Belle scooped up Stone's *epee* by hooking the point of her blade into its hilt.

"Dusty!" she called and flipped the weapon forward.

Catching the flying *epee,* Dusty started down the stairs to the deck and Belle followed him. Finding themselves outnumbered, the last two sailors threw down their cutlasses and surrendered.

"Now maybe somebody'll tell *me* what the hell this's all about," Red growled.

"Secure the prisoners, Red," Dusty answered, by way of explanation. "Then start getting the baggage aboard. How is it, Billy Jack?"

"Hurts like hell, but I'll live," the gangling non-com replied.

"Happen you don't," Dusty said sympathetically, "stay alive until after you help with the prisoners."

With that, Dusty turned and looked around the poop-deck. Seeing Belle disappearing into the cabin, Dusty ordered the wounded men to go down to the main deck and then bounded after her.

## CHAPTER SIXTEEN

# Captain Smee Delivers
# His Cargo

"You dirty, double-dealing, foul hound!" Belle hissed, her *epee* resting its needle-tip on Smee's adam's apple and holding him against the day cabin's wall. "I ought to kill you."

"It—it wasn't of my own free will!" Smee gurgled, eyes bulging in terror. "That Yankee ironclad ran alongside me out beyond sight of land. Had me under its guns. I daren't disobey—"

"So you sold me out!" the girl purred, sounding as menacing as a she-cougar protecting her young.

"No!" Smee howled. "They knew about my cargo. Put a boarding party here and told me if I caused them any trouble, they'd sink me out there without letting anybody get away to tell tales. I had to do what they said."

"So?"

"Stone, he's the captain of the ironclad, and his men came aboard. They locked all my crew who weren't needed to work ship up forward, then stowed the rest away after we dropped anchor. I never told them who you might be. They knew it all along. Stone and his men dressed as civilians. That was why I left the case with the swords out, he couldn't wear his own, didn't dare use a revolver, and wanted a weapon handy without causing suspicion. I had to do what they said, I tell you. I just had to."

"Can you get this ship out of here right away, Captain?" Dusty asked from the door.

"Near enough," Smee agreed.

"Then free your crew and do it."

"But—" Smee began.

"Mister," Dusty growled. "You make me one bit more trouble and I'll kill you where you stand. Then if I can't have the arms for the Confederacy, I'll see that nobody else gets them."

"All I wanted to say was that the ironclad's still laying off shore," Smee quavered. "If she sees us coming out, she'll want to know why."

"Likely," Dusty agreed. "In which case, we'll have to think up some mighty smart answers."

The officer of the watch aboard the U. S. *Sinclair* lifted his speaking trumpet as he watched the *Lancastrian* approach through the gathering darkness.

"*Lancastrian* ahoy!" he bellowed. "Captain Stone, sir!"

Sweat trickled down Smee's face as he prepared to reply. The barrel of Dusty's right-hand Colt bored encouragingly into Smee's ribs.

"Captain Stone took the rebels," Smee called back. "He and his men have gone ashore with their prisoners at Brownsville. He said for you to go in and take him aboard."

Dusty stood at Smee's side and waited for what seemed like a very long time. Aboard the *Sinclair,* the first lieutenant gave a satisfied grunt. Maybe something had happened to change Stone's original plan for returning in the *Lancastrian.* Possibly his captain wanted a show of force on hand to impress the French garrison. Lifting his speaking trumpet, he pointed it towards the other ship.

"All right. Now get the hell out of here; and the next time we see you in our waters, we'll ram you—by accident."

Slowly the two ships parted, the Sinclair heading towards Brownsville and the *Lancastrian* making due west —until out of sight of the other. Then she swung to the south and the waiting *Snow Queen.*

"We brought it off, Dusty," Belle breathed as she came from the captain's night cabin and looked astern to the tiny lights which marked the departing ironclad.

"So far," Dusty agreed. "All we have to do now is find the *Snow Queen,* transfer the arms to her, put Stone and his men ashore, and run the Yankee blockade to land the arms."

Belle smiled and looked at the small—no, she would never think of Dusty Fog as being small—man whose courage, reasoning power and guts had done so much to make her mission a success.

"I've a feeling we'll do it too."

Belle's feeling proved to be correct. After an uneventful voyage, and a narrow escape, the *Snow Queen* slipped through the waters of Atchafalaya Bay one night and delivered a cargo of arms, bought by Yankee gold, to Morgan City.

# WANTED:
## Hard Drivin' Westerns From
# J.T. Edson

J.T. Edson's famous "Floating Outfit" adventure books are on every Western fan's **MOST WANTED** list. Don't miss any of them!

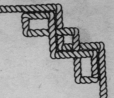

*Blazing heroic adventures
of the gunfighters of the WILD WEST
by Spur Award-winning author*

# LEWIS B. PATTEN

| | | |
|---|---|---|
| _____ | **GIANT ON HORSEBACK** | 0-441-28816-2/$2.50 |
| _____ | **THE GUN OF JESSE HAND** | 0-441-30797-3/$2.50 |
| _____ | **THE RUTHLESS RANGE** | 0-441-74181-9/$2.50 |
| _____ | **THE STAR AND THE GUN** | 0-441-77955-7/$2.50 |

# Raw, fast-action adventure from one of the world's favorite western authors

# MAX BRAND

## writing as Evan Evans

| | | |
|---|---|---|
| 0-515-08571-5 | MONTANA RIDES | $2.50 |
| 0-515-08527-8 | OUTLAW'S CODE | $2.50 |
| 0-515-08528-6 | THE REVENGE OF BROKEN ARROW | $2.75 |
| 0-515-08529-4 | SAWDUST AND SIXGUNS | $2.50 |
| 0-515-08582-0 | STRANGE COURAGE | $2.50 |
| 0-515-08611-8 | MONTANA RIDES AGAIN | $2.50 |
| 0-515-08692-4 | THE BORDER BANDIT | $2.50 |
| 0-515-08711-4 | SIXGUN LEGACY | $2.50 |
| 0-515-08776-9 | SMUGGLER'S TRAIL | $2.50 |
| 0-515-08759-9 | OUTLAW VALLEY | $2.50 |

## Powerful Western Adventure from

# ELMER KELTON

### Winner of the Spur Award and the Western Writers of America Award for Best Western Novel

| | | |
|---|---|---|
| __0-441-05090-5 | **BARBED WIRE** | $2.50 |
| __0-441-06364-0 | **BITTER TRAIL** | $2.50 |
| __0-441-15266-X | **DONOVAN** | $2.50 |
| __0-441-34337-6 | **HOT IRON** | $2.50 |
| __0-441-76068-6 | **SHADOW OF A STAR** | $2.50 |